THE
HORSE SOLDIER

Martin Windrow & Richard Hook

'Here come these fools again!'

*Ensign Macready, British 30th Foot, of French cavalry
charges on the regimental square at Waterloo, 18 June 1815*

'It must be accepted as a principle that the rifle,
effective as it is, cannot replace the effect produced by
the speed of the horse, the magnetism of the charge,
and the terror of cold steel.'

British Army Cavalry Regulations, 1907

Oxford University Press   1986

Oxford University Press, Walton Street, Oxford OX2 6DP

Oxford London
New York Toronto Melbourne Auckland
Petaling Jaya Singapore Hong Kong Tokyo
Delhi Bombay Calcutta Madras Karachi
Nairobi Dar es Salaam Cape Town

and associated companies in
Beirut Berlin Ibadan Nicosia

Oxford is a trade mark of Oxford University Press
© Richard Hook and Martin Windrow 1986

British Library Cataloguing in Publication Data

Windrow, Martin
 The horse soldier.–(Rebuilding the past)
 1. Cavalry–History–Juvenile literature
 I. Title II. Hook, Richard III. Series
 357'.1'09 UE15

ISBN 0–19–273157–2

Phototypeset by Oxford Publishing Services, Oxford

Printed in Hong Kong

Contents

The Horse in War

No other animal has been as closely woven into the long adventure of human history as the horse; and no other animal has played a serious part in man's warfare. On the back of a swift-running horse a man becomes more than a man: he is twice as tall as other men, and three times as fast. He can herd his cattle over huge distances; run down his prey for the cooking-pot; and fall upon distant enemies without warning. Man has rewarded the horse for its great heart, its beauty and its obedience with a special kind of love. This has not prevented him slaughtering horses in uncounted millions.

The ancestors of the modern horse were stocky ponies which emerged from the evolutionary maze about one million years ago, on the plains of North America. By about 50,000 years ago the wandering herds had crossed the land bridge which then linked Alaska and Russia, and were spreading over the whole landmass of Asia and Europe. If they had not made that journey, history might have been very different: for about 10,000 years ago a mysterious epidemic seems to have wiped out the American herds completely, and the horse was not seen on the prairies again until the arrival of the Spanish explorers in the 16th century.

Their cave-paintings and bone-dumps prove that early men hunted and ate the horse just like any other animal. The earliest evidence of horse-riding comes from crude carvings dating from some time after 3,000 BC. Men probably used the first tamed horses to drag sledges or primitive carts; but at some unknown date, somewhere on the great, empty Asian plains which stretch almost 4,000 miles from the Danube to the heart of China, a man discovered the possibilities of riding.

The nameless herdsman or hunter who proved the point must have been a man of extraordinary courage and patience, to say nothing of his imaginative vision. A wild horse is strong, unpredictable, lightning-fast, and often savagely dangerous. It quivers on the edge of panic flight at the first warning from its superb eyes and keen nose. Above all, it hates the sensation of anything on its back — for the good evolutionary reason that for a million years anything that jumped on its back usually intended to eat it.

Chariots and Cavalry

The horse first appeared as man's companion in war yoked to a chariot. This light war-cart, carrying a driver and one or two spearmen or archers, played an important part in Middle Eastern history during the 2,000 years before Christ. Although its use stretched from China to Britain over those twenty centuries, the chariot had serious limitations, and proved in the long run to be a military 'blind alley'. Far cheaper, far easier to find and to train in large numbers, and far more versatile was the single man astride a single horse.

The cavalryman gave the war-leader the priceless gift of mobility, both 'strategic' and 'tactical'. The simplest explanation of these two strands of military skill is to say that strategy is the business of moving armies across the map, and tactics the business of moving men around the battlefield, in such a way as to gain the greatest advantage over the enemy. True cavalry was certainly known in Mesopotamia by the 10th century BC. By that time it had been understood for hundreds of years that the breed of horses could be improved by proper care: by careful stabling and grooming, and by feeding with grain instead of leaving

Most of our knowledge of ancient Middle Eastern use of the horse and chariot in war comes from surviving carvings. From these we learn that (*left*) Assyrian cavalry of the 9th century BC rode in pairs, with one man handling the reins of both horses while the other used his bow. The archers who rode in chariots carried quivers of extra arrows slung on the side of the chariot (*centre left*); and other chariot crews included shield-bearers who protected the archers and charioteers (*centre right*). At *far right* we see the emergence of the true horse-archer.

the herds to graze as best they could.

Very early in man's relationship with the horse, far back in the days of the chariot, a link was forged between the keeping of horses for war, and the most wealthy and powerful landowners. Raising horses in any numbers requires territory and men, and therefore money and power. It is not too fanciful to remember, as well, the personal feeling of superiority which a man enjoys when looking down from a saddle. This connection between horses and aristocracy has survived to our own times.

The horse played a central part in human warfare from pre-Christian times until the First World War. Modern weapons of mass destruction have released the horse at last from the ancient partnership, which cost the horse so dear. But the soldier on horseback is still a powerful image in our memory, woven deep into our legends. He lasted for 3,000 years; he has not yet been obsolete for a hundred. There are still many old men alive who rode into battle during the last years of the cavalryman's usefulness.

Many countries still celebrate the old images by keeping a mounted ceremonial bodyguard to add a romantic echo to occasions of state pageantry. To stand by the roadside as they jingle past — massive, gleaming, proud, and so far above our heads — is to be reminded of how powerful and frightening the horse-soldier must have been in the days of his glory. In some periods he dominated the battlefield, herding terrified foot soldiers at his will; in others, some advance in weaponry left him dashing himself bloodily against the rocks of stubborn infantry. But in all periods, during thirty long centuries, he was a man to be reckoned with. No foot soldier dared ignore him, even in his periods of decline; and for many generations of fighting men, it was the horseman who was the true lord of the battlefield.

Scopasis of the Royal Scyths, 500 BC

As the loose skein of Scythian hunters breasted a slight, deceptive fold in the grassy plain, the hind they were tracking sprang up almost under the hooves of Scopasis' pony. The sturdy little beast missed his step, snorting with surprise — and with a triumphant whoop Palakus, the boy's father, shouldered his own pony past his son, already nocking a reed arrow to the string of his short, powerful bow. Guiding his mount expertly with his knees, he hurtled up alongside the deer before it had properly got into its stride. Away to the right, Scopasis' brothers were still wheeling their mounts in a cloud of dust as their father's first arrow sank deeply behind the quarry's shoulder. A second had been drawn, nocked and shot between the hind's ribs before it fell, crashing and sliding to the grass. The other riders came shouting up, springing from their saddle-pads in a noisy, good-humoured crowd as Palakus straightened up over his kill, his knife dripping.

'You'll have to school your ponies better than that for the war-trail, boy!' But his father's grin was affectionate: Palakus knew that Scopasis was as fine a natural rider as any 17-year-old who had been lifted on to his first pony before he could walk. The bearded chieftain darted a bloodstained hand out, and wiped a salty red smear across his son's lips.

'There — she *should* have been yours, anyway!'

With a rueful laugh, Scopasis drew his long knife and knelt to help his father paunch the kill. He was irritated with himself for fumbling like that — but nothing could really spoil his pleasure on a day like this.

Spring on the steppes

It was the middle of June, and the knowledge that spring on the steppes would soon be over made it all the sweeter. For weeks now the sun had blazed down every day from the huge blue bowl of the sky, and the endless grasslands had been splashed with wildflowers. In ten or twenty days now, the heat would dry and yellow the silvery waves of grass; the iris and tulip, the white whitlow and blue sage would die back; and the sweet wind that seemed to blow from the ends of the earth would turn hot and dusty. Then it would be time to break the spring camp, and take the herds and flocks to the low river valleys where they could fatten on the lusher grass, and where the tents and waggons could cluster in the cool shade of willows and birches.

But for now, the open steppe was Scopasis' playground. Here he could race his ponies all day, shouting for the sheer joy of speed and strength. Here he could spend all day hunting with his brothers and his mighty father — and in June the game was so plentiful that even the blinded slaves who milked the mares could go greasy-chinned and belching to their blankets, every night of the month.

As they jogged easily back to camp, swapping the boasts and lies which complete every hunter's pleasure, Scopasis could feel the beginning of that delicious tiredness which only comes to those who spend all day stretching their muscles in the open air. His belly was reminding him that he had not eaten since snatching a barley-cake and a handful of cheese in the first light of dawn, as he ran to catch and unhobble his pony. He closed his eyes, and imagined the venison already stewing: bubbling in the cauldron with onions, and garlic, and beans to thicken the wonderful juices. The smell would come wafting over to the pony herd while he rubbed down his mount with handfuls of long grass, and watered him, and left him hobbled to graze round the camp. The younger boys would be trying to snatch gobblets straight from the pot, and the women would be laughing and scolding. And after the food, there would be stories. . .

Warrior dreams

He loved to lounge by the fire on a thick pile of rugs, included at last among the men after the long, frustrating years of childhood. The fiery kumiss would be passed around the fire; and, if Palakus was in an expansive mood, he might call for a skin of his favourite Greek trade-wine, heavy and purple, and for the marvellous silver and gold bowl he had bought in Olbia, far to the south on the ocean shore.

As a little boy, Scopasis had loved to hear the old legends from his mother, or from one of his father's other wives: the tales of Colaxis, first-father of the Paralatai — the Royal Scyths — who had plucked the golden plough, yoke, axe and cup out of the ghostly flames to earn the favour of the great goddess Tabiti. He had shuddered deliciously at travellers' stories of monsters and mysteries: of the Neurian werewolves, and the cannibals who lived north of the steppes. When he was a little older he had sniggered at tales of the unspeakably immoral habits of the Agathyrsi tribe. But now he was a man, and he gloried in tales of war.

He had never ridden the Red Trail himself, and he burned with eagerness to join the brotherhood of true warriors. Every evening of his life he dreamed of his first kill. He imagined his father standing before him, glorious in his bronze helmet and shimmering scale armour, proudly chanting the ritual words as Scopasis drank the blood of his first slain enemy, and tied the reeking scalp to his bridle. Then he would be able to cut his hair, like a warrior; and in time, to grow a beard. (His chin was depressingly smooth at the moment — like a girl's, newly cleaned with cypress-pulp and frankincense. The beard might take a little time. . .)

Scythian coin bearing the name of King Atai, who fell in battle at the age of 90, fighting the Macedonians in 339 BC. Typically, the coin shows the two things most important to a Scyth — the horse and the bow. We have evidence that they bred three main types of mount. Noblemen favoured a large, reddish-coloured gelding of Iranian stock as a warhorse; the smaller, stockier pony was the all-purpose mount; and a very small breed was kept for eating.

He saw himself in his daydreams as a great chief like Palakus, riding a tall, red Ferghana gelding, with a fortune in gold jingling on the harness. He would take six beautiful young wives, and sire a dozen strong sons, and set his ear-brand on five hundred ponies. His armour would be made by Greek smiths, and would glitter in the sunset like captive fire, as he presided over the butchering of prisoners below the Hill of the Sword. . . Scopasis of the Paralatai would lead his thundering hordes far to the south where men had rooms full of gold, and lakes full of wine; and stumbled around on their own feet, like oxen to be slaughtered, in the streets of their strange stone camps. . .

But the wine-bowl was circulating, and his father was telling Scopasis' favourite story: of the Great War, twelve years gone, when Palakus had ridden with King Idanthyrsus against the horde of Darius the Persian, and had left the bones of thousands to whiten on the endless sea of grass.

The War of the Stinging Fly

Darius the Achaemenid had spread the shadow of his throne across an empire stretching from the sands of Egypt to the hills of the Indian frontier. Now his eyes were turning westwards; but before he moved against Greece, he determined to clear his northern flank of any threat from the Scythians, who had raided as they pleased for generations.

He had a bridge of boats built across the Hellespont, and led into Europe an army of hundreds of thousands of men. Smashing through the hillmen of Thrace, he reached the mighty Danube; and there again he had a bridge built by lashing together scores of ships, side by side. Across this wooden road he led his horde, northwards and eastwards on to the Pontic steppe — the grasslands of the Scyths.

Unable to persuade neighbouring tribes to fight at his side, King Idanthyrsus knew that he could not face such a mighty enemy face to face — but he had no need to. The pony, the bow, and the endless plains themselves were his weapons; and he used them well. He split his army in two: the one half he sent west, to meet the Persians on their road. The Scythian riders were to raid and entice the Persians, drawing them ever eastwards but never letting them get close enough for a pitched battle. Sweeping in on their agile ponies, loosing a few volleys of arrows, then sweeping away again, they were to be the stinging flies which lured the maddened bull of Persia further and further from safety. As they fell back before him they fired the grazing and spoiled the wells; every animal for a day's ride on each side of the Persians' path was killed or driven off. As the weeks passed, the Persian host became ever hungrier, thirstier, and more tired. Scythian raiders shot down their foraging parties; and sickness began to stalk the camp-grounds.

Idanthyrsus himself, with the other half of the Scythians' strength, marched parallel to the Persians on their northern flank. Further north still, the women and children, waggons and herds moved far from the path of danger. Keeping between them and the enemy, Idanthyrsus delicately herded the Persians back into the waterless, burnt-out strip of grassland to the east every time they showed signs of turning northwards. Darius was never able to close with the Scythians, and never able to judge their strength; he saw only the whirling raiding-parties, always falling back to avoid his ponderous blows — and always leading him deeper into the frightening emptiness of the plains.

At last, the Scythians seemed ready to stand and fight. The day came when Darius could draw up his drooping regiments in battle array, facing the quicksilver horse-archers of Idanthyrsus across the grassy plain. But at the last moment, a hare started up in panic from the grass between the two armies — and with a hoot of excitement, the whole Scythian host raced off after it, more interested in the chase than in fighting the Persians. Darius understood the lesson: and decided, finally, to turn for home. His army faced a long, terrible retreat, with the triumphant Scythians tearing at their flanks like wolves. Countless thousands of Persians died on that march, of wounds, starvation and disease. Darius the Great was forced to accept the lesson that a highly mobile army of horse-archers, with limitless territory to range over and no fixed strongholds to defend, could always dictate the course of a war by refusing battle until it suited them.

'They will eat your sons and daughters'

The riders of Palakus' clan never tired of the story; and as their chief brought it to a close tonight, they cheered and clashed their wine-cups. Two of the older men began a furious argument over which of them had brought back the greater number of severed heads strung to his pony's harness. Palakus called one of his wives to bring him his favourite cup, and the warriors shouted anew as it was lifted from its beautifully decorated leather bag: the polished skull of a Medean officer, his cranium neatly sawn off and a golden cup fitted into his brain-pan. Scopasis stood behind his father's shoulder, and carefully poured from the wineskin. Palakus smiled at the boy, and raised the grisly trophy.

'Never fear, cub — there'll be wars aplenty for you, too!' He drank deeply, and wiped his bearded lips with a richly embroidered sleeve.

'Those accursed Sauromatai, now — they'll be sticking their snouts into our grazing more boldly each summer, depend upon it. Their eastern steppes are poorly watered: the dogs will be after our grass for their herds. It'll be up to you and your brothers to greet them with proper gifts . . . Paralatai arrows, boy, sharp and straight, at 400 paces!

'And always remember, boy — you must never let them get you boxed up close. The Sauromatai wear more armour than we do, and hang it round those damned big horses of theirs, too. If they catch you somewhere you can't wheel and scatter, and get in among you with their long lances and two-handed swords — then they'll go over you like a flooding river.

'A Scyth's the master of anything that runs — as long as he's got space to float like a hawk. Stand like a stupid farmer, and you'll die like one!'

As the night darkened around the firelit camp, Scopasis began to nod off in his nest of rugs. The warriors were singing now, an ancient song, and Scopasis sleepily mouthed the words as he drifted off. They were supposed to come from some outlandish priest-chant, brought back to the Sea of Grass by riders who had crossed the southern mountains centuries before — a chant of fear at the coming of the Scythians:

'*Their quivers are like open graves . . . They will eat your harvest and bread, they will eat your sheep and oxen, they will eat your grapes and figs — they will eat your sons and daughters. . .*'

The Scythians were a blood-thirsty people, given to orgies of drink and violence; they are known to have taken scalps and heads from slain enemies as a matter of course, and one prisoner in every hundred was sacrificed to their war-god by dismemberment in front of a rough altar — a brushwood or earthen mound topped with a sword.

The Scythians' own burial rites were hardly less grisly. When a king died his embalmed corpse would be paraded around his tribal camps, while his people slashed themselves with knives in a frenzy of mourning. He would then be laid in his grave, surrounded by his riches and by the bodies of sacrificed slaves and horses — sometimes in great numbers. A high mound would be raised over the grave. Later, to guard their king forever, numbers of other men and horses would be sacrificed and roughly embalmed, and their corpses arranged on wooden frames in a circle all round the King's grave-mound. Despite these terrifying guardians, most graves were later robbed.

The Pony and the Bow

The Scythians, who are first mentioned in 7th-century Assyrian texts, were the first true cavalry army in European history. They came to dominate the plains north and east of the Black Sea between about 700 and 300 BC; and they ranged far wider than that as mercenaries and marauders, leaving traces of their passing from Poland to Egypt.

They lived as nomads, following their pony herds and their flocks along the path of the best pasture from season to season. They seem to have demanded regular 'taxes' from the farming communities and trading cities around the fringes of their 'sea of grass'; and they levied foot soldiers for some of their campaigns from among these settled peoples. But the pony was the basis of their wealth, their way of life, and their war-tactics. Every man who could provide himself with a pony and a bow was a warrior; and since the Scythians became very rich, they seem to have been able to put tens of thousands of riders into the field.

Brave, skilled and tireless horsemen, they covered great distances, travelling light. Generations of herding and hunting had polished their skills with horse and bow until they were able to keep enemies at arm's length, weakening and tormenting them with clouds of arrows until the Scythians chose to pick the time and place for battle. The short, powerful Central Asian bow, made of wood, bone and sinew glued together, was said to have a range of more than 400 yards — an enormous distance, if true. Skeletons have been found with slim, superbly-made bronze arrowheads embedded an inch into the solid bone.

In the early centuries few Scythians wore any armour, apart from an iron-faced belt to protect the belly, and perhaps a stiffened leather cap. (Their wealthy chiefs bought iron and bronze armour from

Greek traders.) They were masters of hit-and-run fighting: swooping in to deliver showers of arrows and javelins, then darting out of the reach of their less agile enemies. In the Scythian horse-archers we see a classic demonstration of the value of mobility in war.

It is interesting that some of their later grave-mounds contain complete suits of armour: hundreds of metal 'scales' sewn to leather jerkins, helmets and leggings. This heavy war-gear is the last thing a mounted archer would want. It suggests that by the 4th century BC part of their army was fighting in disciplined formations, as 'shock' cavalry. An account of a battle in 310 BC describes just these tactics: a core of heavy, armoured horsemen armed with spears and shields smashed through the enemy ranks, supported and followed by the usual loose mob of unarmoured archers.

This type of charge has been dismissed by some historians as impossible for riders without the support of stirrups and high-backed saddles — and the Scythians had neither. But, although they may not have been able to brace a lance under their arms, like medieval knights, many horse soldiers in ancient times certainly fought as true 'shock' cavalry — so we must assume that they were better at riding without stirrups than modern historians are!

The Scythians faded from history as mysteriously as they had come. The 'Sauromatai' — Sarmatians, from east of the River Don — slowly squeezed them west and south; and by 100 BC only a tiny remnant of Scopasis' people were left, living in the Crimea. They left us their superb gold and silver grave-goods; and the dim memory of the first of many armies of horse-archers out of the East which have terrified Europe throughout history.

(*Opposite*) A Scythian horse-archer of the 6th century BC brandishes his sword after taking a trophy of war. Metalware found in Scythian graves gives us a good idea of their costume and equipment. The combined quiver and bowcase, called by the Greeks a *gorytos*, was very common.

(*Below*) 4th century Scythian heavy cavalryman wearing one of the scale-armour suits found in a few grave-mounds.

An Infantry Landscape: Greece, 500–340 BC

By about a hundred years after the war in which the Scythians beat off the Persian invasion of their heartland, some of the nomads from the steppes were taking service as mercenary soldiers with the armies of the civilised Greek city-states far to the south of their home range. There they fought on battlefields shaped by a military tradition about as different from their own as they could imagine. Greece was the cradle of the heavy, armoured infantryman, fighting with spear and shield in tight formation.

The reason why the horse played such a small part in Greek warfare of the 'classical' period between the 6th and mid-4th centuries BC was a simple matter of landscape.

On the northern steppes horses breed naturally. There were plenty of horses, and plenty of space for them to feed. Given the nomadic habits of the steppe tribes, and the need to drive their flocks and herds over huge distances, it was natural for them to tame the horses for their use.

But in Greece four-fifths of the countryside is mountainous. There is very little land where food may be grown, and every acre is important. With millions of square miles of free grazing, and hundreds of thousands of horses running free, it was natural for the steppe peoples to develop as wanderers and horsemen. In the valleys between Greece's stony ribs it was equally natural for the people to develop as farmers, living in small defensive communities behind village walls, and clinging to the few score acres of riverbank, drained marsh or hillside orchard on which they depended for their livelihood.

Distances were not great, and few people had any reason to travel far by land. Although riding-horses were bred in Greece, they were not available to enough of the population for any habit of cavalry fighting to grow up. Breeding horse herds needs a lot of open grassland; and the only area in Greece suitable for large-scale ranching was the Boeotian Plain, most of which was far too valuable for growing grain to feed human beings to be wasted on stock-raising. The scarcity of horses made them more expensive in Greece, and horsemen were usually the wealthier aristocrats. Some of them rode horses into battle, but too few of them for cavalry tactics to be studied seriously.

The Greek way of warfare is described in our book *The Footsoldier* (OUP, 1983). All but the poorest

A Thracian mercenary horseman dressed in a colourful cloak and a fur cap and armed with light javelins: he is reconstructed from this vase painting. Useful for scouting, these 'cowboys' could not hurt formed-up armoured infantry. Even Xenophon, a cavalry leader, told his infantrymen that the only advantage enjoyed by the cavalry was that they could run away more easily!

of a town's citizens would muster in time of war, each man providing his own armour and weapons. Formed into disciplined blocks of men, each unit would pack tight against the next to make a single long battle-line of overlapped shields and bristling spearheads, some eight men deep by several hundred yards long. They would crash into the enemy line head on; and the day was decided by the strength and staying-power of spearmen fighting face to face in a murderous press of bodies.

This massed formation, the *phalanx*, was supported by both lightly-armed infantry, and by small numbers of Greek or mercenary cavalry. But it was the *phalanx* which governed the tactics and the outcome of the battle: the horsemen were only used to scout, or to skirmish on the flanks in the steep, wooded hills to make sure the enemy did not slip around the main infantry force.

Apart from the Scythians, the main sources of these mercenary cavalry were the plains of Thessaly, a wild frontier region north of the main Greek city-states; and Thrace, an even wilder region, whose inhabitants were regarded by the Greeks as little better than animals. The Thracian and Thessalian riders who fought in Greek wars were lightly armed and unarmoured, and were still used mainly as scouts. But it was from this northern border region that a new power threatened Greece, and overcame her, in the middle years of the 4th century BC: Macedonia.

A new kind of army

Macedonia was ruled between 359 and 336 BC by an extraordinary man, King Philip II. With great fore-sight and energy, he built his wild hillmen into an army the equal of anything in Greece. In the southern states, infantry armour was now a good deal lighter than it had been; so Philip put his infantry *phalanx* into heavier armour, and trained them to use longer spears. He also supported them in battle by raising a really effective force of armoured cavalry equipped with lances. He gave great estates to aristocrats from all over the Greek world, encouraging them to raise horses and train cavalrymen to fight in a new way: to charge together in disciplined groups, smashing through the lines of enemy infantry with their long lances. Nothing like this had been seen before in Greece.

The combination of a heavier infantry *phalanx*, and a disciplined force of 'shock' cavalry, won Philip the rule of the whole of Greece by 388 BC. He was assassinated soon afterwards; but he left a 20-year-old son who was an even more astonishingly gifted general than his father: Alexander, called the Great, who conquered most of the known world in the twelve years which followed. And he conquered it from the saddle — the king himself led the heavy cavalry which

Reconstruction of a 5th-century Persian cavalryman. Some 8,000 mounted archers and javelineers took part in the invasion of Greece in 480 BC, when the Greeks faced Eastern light horse tactics for the first time. At the battle of Plataea in 479 BC the cavalry charged many times, causing heavy losses: but, under cover of their shields and helmets, the Greek heavy infantry held out, and their steadiness won the day.

formed the crack corps of the army.

This bringing together of trained infantry and trained cavalry, each fighting in the way that had proved most effective, was an important milestone. It was a 'modern' way of conducting wars. To under-stand what a shock the Macedonian tactics were to the Greek world on which they burst so suddenly, we must remember that because of the Greek tradition of fighting only on foot, no infantry drills or tactics had been worked out to deal with cavalry who charged fearlessly, instead of swirling round the edges of the battlefield and fighting each other, in the manner of the mercenary light horsemen. Persian horse-archers and javelineers had given the Greeks a shock during an invasion in 480 BC; but this one isolated lesson had been forgotten, and the city-states settled down into their old, conservative tradition. The Macedonians made that tradition obsolete in a single generation.

Agathon, Tetrarch of Companion Cavalry, 331 BC

'Hold your ranks! Hold steady! What are you — a bunch of Thracians?! Wait for the trumpet, and *hold*, curse you!'

Agathon's throat, choked with the gritty dust which hung over the battlefield of Gaugamela like dirty yellow fog, felt as if it was going to crack as he twisted round over his horse's rump and bellowed at his skittish troopers. They angled out behind him on both sides in a solid wedge of purple tunics and bronze helmets, their slim lances wavering and rattling above them like saplings in a storm. Their mounts tossed their heads and pawed the dirt uneasily, fighting the cruelly spiked bits. At the back of the troop Agathon could hear his three sergeants adding their curses to his. The troopers were the cream of King Alexander's army, and after more than three years of campaigning they were soldiers that the gods would be proud to command. Nevertheless, although they were in no real danger, it was hard to sit like statues and watch a wave of Persian chariots rumbling and careering across the

plain straight towards them, the razor-sharp scythes on the wheels glittering evilly. If the chariots ever *did* manage to get in among the horses, the carnage would be hideous.

They didn't, of course. While they were still far out on the bare, packed dirt of the plain between Macedonian and Persian battle-lines, the doll-like figures of charioteers and spearmen began to topple out in the roiling dust. The thick line of archers and javelineers Alexander had spread along the front of his right flank cavalry soaked up the chariot charge like a sponge. A few moments later the last of the war-carts went bouncing crazily past a hundred paces to the left of the squadron, its driver dead and pinioned to the platform by arrows. The ranks of the Royal Shield-bearers infantry regiment moved smartly into close order to make a wide corridor for its passage. The forty-odd troopers of Agathon's Tetrarchy of the Bottiaean Squadron of Companion Cavalry settled down again, each man straining for the first notes of the trumpet which would signal the attack.

At least the dust hid the vast Persian battle-line from their sight now. They knew it outnumbered the Greeks and Macedonians four or five to one: but they preferred not to be reminded of the fact by having to stare at it in these last, stomach-tightening moments before the charge. Especially the elephants. . . They had been told that elephants were not really dangerous, if you kept the cavalry horses beyond reach of their maddening smell; but all the same, to actually *see* the monsters, as tall as a house, drawn up in front of the Persian centre. . . !

Alexander's veterans

Agathon concentrated on his own job and his own men: there was no point in thinking ahead. He sidestepped his horse out from its position at the point of the wedge, and turned it to have a last look over his troop, forcing himself to ignore the din of battle over on the left wing of the army. The gods alone knew what was happening away in the dust-clouds there! His troop was well up to strength, considering. There were still a few gaps in the rear rank; but he had received some replacements when they were at Memphis four months ago, and the army's pool of remounts had provided the horses he needed to make up for those which had broken down on the march. Whenever they could, the cavalry marched on foot and led their beasts; but these damned stony Asian plains were murderous on unshod hooves.

Agathon's horse, in its full parade harness: the handsome pantherskin saddle cloth was a mark of the Companion Cavalry, like their purple tunics, and yellow cloaks bordered with purple. The regiment was recruited from wealthy land-owning families, and even troopers were men of means. Each had a groom to care for his horses, which the trooper provided himself; the army kept a 'pool' of spare mounts, and issued them to replace casualties.

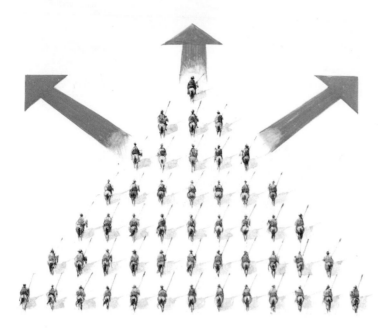

Agathon's troop: he rides at the point, with three sergeants at the ends and middle of the rear rank. Four troops made up a 200-man squadron; King Alexander had seven regionally-raised Companion squadrons on his Asian campaign, totalling 1,400 men.

The extra 300-strong Royal Squadron was led by the king in person. The wedge formation allowed the Companions to change direction, half-left or half-right, without losing the advantage of their deep, disciplined arrangement of ranks.

The men were in good heart, though naturally tense. Some met his eyes and gave a tight grin; others gave their young officer only a stiff nod, and looked down, suddenly busy with their reins or the laces of their breastplates. Even Philonedes, the troop clown, had to run his tongue over dry lips before giving Agathon a lop-sided smile. As usual, the fool wasn't wearing his stiff linen and leather breastplate. He hated the restriction of it; and boasted that he had come through the battles of the River Granicus and Issus without a scratch, and that it would be impolite to the god Enyalios, his protector, to start hedging his bets by wearing it now. Philonedes was the son of one of Agathon's father's richest tenants, back on the huge family estates south over the lake from Pella. The two young men had grown up together, and Philonedes traded on the fact shamelessly.

Seeing the familiar face brought home back into Agathon's mind with a sudden clarity. How long ago, how far away it was — that glorious morning, three and a half years back, when the godlike young Alexander had led them out on the first march of their campaign to conquer the greatest empire in the world.

Agathon had marched and ridden all over the stony uplands of Asia Minor; then far, far to the south, along the edge of the sea, through Palestine, to the long, horrible siege of Tyre. He had ridden the burning white sands of Egypt, accompanying Alexander to the strange temple at the oasis far beyond Memphis. He had seen friends die, of wounds and plague and bad water; and he had lost count of the enemies he had killed himself. And still Alexander led them on — gay, laughing, hard as steel; never out-generalled, never shamed, and always with a joke and a clap on the shoulder for his Companions. They would follow him still, wherever he chose to lead. When a god beckons, you don't ask why: you follow.

A flash of pink crossing in front of him jerked Agathon's attention back to the present. A Thracian scout, kicking his horse towards the squadron commander: that meant orders. Far off to the right, at the head of the Royal Squadron on the furthest advanced horn of the whole army, Alexander would be vaulting up on to old Oxhead's back, shouting commands. It was not hard to guess what they would be.

The King's gambit

It was his old trick, and it still worked. When he led the army forward that morning, Alexander had slanted his own right wing of cavalry further and further off to the right. Here the King sat, his whole army slanting away behind his left shoulder, while his cunningly-placed flank guards of mixed Greek cavalry and light infantry had driven off a massed attack by heavy, armoured horses from Scythia and Bactria. The chariots, too, had been countered. Now Alexander would turn inwards, and strike at the heart of Darius' front line. His move out to the right had forced the Persians to stretch their front, too, to avoid being outflanked: and a gap had opened up between their left wing and centre. That chink in the vast, multi-coloured horde of Asian troops was the target he would strike with his spearhead of Companions. Agathon took up his station again, and gripped his smooth, cornel-wood lance. As he gentled his nervous mount, the first braying call came through the dusty air from the squadron commander's trumpeter: '*Left incline! . . . Charge!*'

'*Alalalalalai!*' Howling the Macedonian battle-cry, Agathon's troop followed their young officer's silver-wreathed helmet through the dust and into the heart of the milling, white-turbanned Medean infantry. Agathon gripped his slim, shivering lance with both hands in an underarm hold, and stabbed frantically at the first dark face which snarled up at him through the confusion. His point skewered through an up-flung wicker shield, and he kicked his horse onward, swinging his arm down and back to pull the lance free of his unseen victim. Arrows hissed past him: behind him he heard screams of pain — not all of them from horses. He snatched a look back, and saw Philonedes' riderless horse rearing, wild-eyed. *Philonedes! . . . No time for that now. . .* He faced the enemy again, and surged on into the thick of the Persians.

Hannibal at Cannae: the Destroyer of Legions

After Alexander's death at 32, his empire (and his army) broke up into squabbling factions. The next great leader to make imaginative use of cavalry was Hannibal Barca, the Carthaginian. Carthage was a great sea and land power based in Tunisia, which held off the spreading domination of Rome for 120 years, and inflicted on Rome some of her worst-ever defeats. Hannibal was an all-round master of tactics, and a brilliant leader: he kept a multi-national army in the field against Rome for 15 years, in North Africa, Spain, and in Italy itself. His victory over a stronger Roman army at Cannae in 216 BC showed a far more flexible and controlled use of cavalry than even Alexander achieved:

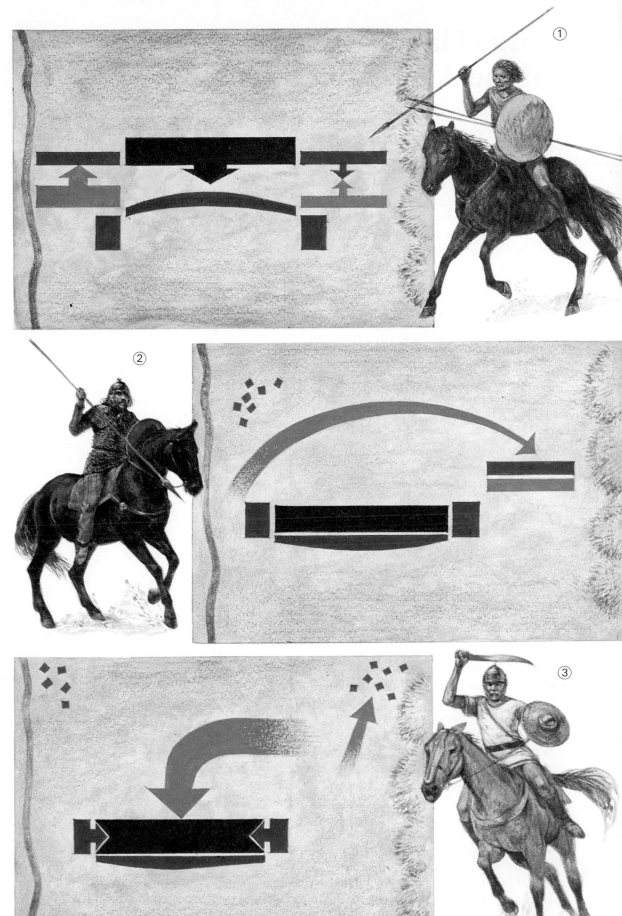

1 Hannibal's light infantry, weaker than the Roman legions facing them, form a crescent; two strong *phalanxes* of the best, armoured infantry are held back behind the flanks. Numidian mounted javelineers manoeuvre on right wing to hold attention of Roman left wing cavalry. Strong Celtic and Spanish horse, on Hannibal's left wing, smash through Roman right wing cavalry. (*Right:* Numidian horseman.)

2 Hannibal's light infantry centre is pressed back by the legions. Celtic and Spanish horse, with remarkable discipline, regroup and ride right across behind Romans, joining Numidians and driving Roman left wing cavalry off the field. (*Left:* Celtic horseman.)

3 Once again the Celts and Spaniards regroup; and ride against the rear of the Roman infantry. Caught on all sides, the Romans are destroyed: of 75,000 men, 50,000 fall and 15,000 are captured. (*Right:* Spanish horseman.)

At Cannae, Hannibal's cavalry demonstrated the essence of good mounted troops: the ability to charge, fight, form up, and attack a second objective, according to orders and under discipline.

Titus Flavius Bassus of the Ala Noricorum,
AD 95

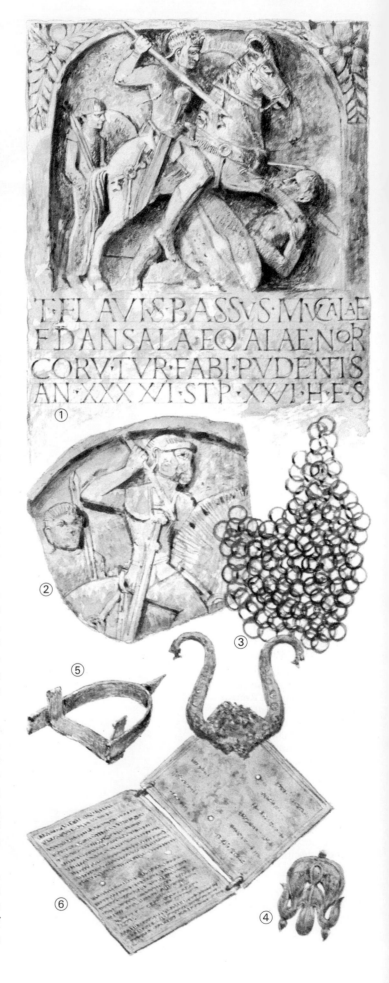

Titus woke at the first note of the trumpet. After 25 years in the army, he had the old campaigner's trick of coming instantly awake and alert as soon as his eyes opened; but forcing his ageing joints to push him to his feet after a short, dreary night spent wrapped in a cloak on the damp ground was another thing entirely. Chilled and stiff, the 46-year-old trooper came creaking and shivering to his knees. Spring was coming, but down on these low-lying flats on the east bank of the Rhine the nights were still foggy and cold. He caught his breath, and coughed.

The first, uninviting grey glimmer was only just beginning to outline the black bulk of the forested hills to the east as the 30-odd troopers of the Noricum Horse stirred into grumbling life under their dew-drenched cloaks. They had slept huddled among the huts of a small farm somewhere on the ten-mile-wide strip of fertile valley bottom between the great Rhine to the west, and the reaching fingers of the wooded hills to the east. Although this eastern bank was officially beyond Rome's Rhine frontier, it had been patrolled regularly for years. Tame Germans had drifted down from the hills to make farms and villages, tempted by trade and by the protection of the nearby west bank garrisons.

Titus, stumbling on stiff legs, made for the gleam of light marking the doorway of the main hut. He craved something warm in his belly, and had in mind to sweet-talk the farmer's woman out of some milk to heat in his mess-tin, perhaps with ration-bread crumbled into it to make a comforting mush. But even as he reached the hut he had a sinking feeling that there would be no breakfast today.

His troop commander, Decurion Flavius Pudens, was standing in the splash of light by the doorway, already fastening his helmet as he shot questions at an unfamiliar, travel-strained trooper. A lathered, blowing horse was tethered by the hut. Titus was still trying to think of a way to slip past the officer when Pudens turned and shouted for his trumpeter. The notes of 'Saddle-up' sent Titus stumbling for his kit, cursing with frustration.

Five minutes later he was in the horse lines, fumbling at old Swallow's girth buckle with cold fingers. As bad-tempered as its rider, the horse spitefully tried to blow its belly out against the pull of the strap, and was rewarded with a bony knee in the

'Reconstructing' Titus

is to some extent possible, since his tombstone was found in Germany: unlike the other soldiers whose stories we imagine in this book, he was a real person. The stone (**1**) tells us that he was the son of Mucala, from Dansala in Thrace; that he died aged 46, in his 26th year of service as a trooper in the *Ala Noricorum*, in the *turma* or troop of Flavius Pudens.

The auxiliary infantry and cavalry (all Roman cavalry were auxiliaries) were raised from non-citizens in newly conquered provinces; their total strength roughly equalled that of the heavy infantry legions of Roman citizens. Auxiliaries usually held frontier posts; legions were often based further back, on strategic routes. Many Roman cavalrymen were Gauls or Thracians, who had long traditions of horsemanship. They were only paid about two-thirds as much as legionaries; but the citizenship rights awarded on discharge brought many legal, tax and career advantages to them and their descendants.

Cavalry helmets of this time often had embossed 'hair' as skull decoration (*right*). In place of the legionary's plate armour, large semi-cylindrical shield and javelins, the trooper had a ring-mail shirt, an oval shield, and a thrusting-spear; his sword was longer, giving the greater reach a horseman needed. The tombstone of another *Ala Noricorum* trooper (**2**) shows the 'cape' of doubled mail at the shoulder, attached by a chest hook. Mail and hooks have been found (**3**) as have harness decorations (**4**) and spurs (**5**) and even a leather saddle with four stiffened 'horns' (*right*). The type of bronze diploma (**6**) which Titus would have received if he had lived is most useful to historians. It lists all units in that province which discharged time-expired men on a given day, helping us build up a picture of the deployment of different regiments.

Cavalry *alae* had 16 *turmae* or troops of about 30 men each. A posting as a regimental commander — *praefectus* — was much sought after by Roman officers.

side. Its breath came out in a great steaming *whuff*! as Titus fastened the buckle of the suddenly loosened girth. All around him was a familiar, half-seen bustle of men and horses: the shuffling and blowing and stamping of the beasts, the monotonous cursing of men harried by impatient officers, the creak and jingle of harness, and the warm, comforting smell of horseflesh.

As he chopped his arm forward in command, and led his gummy-eyed troop off over the dark grasslands at a smart canter, Decurion Flavius Pudens smelled not horses, but action.

Policing the frontier

In the dark of each moon for four months now, German tribesmen from the secret depths of the hills had come stalking down on to these cultivated riverside flats to kill and rob. Although he had no official responsibility, the governor of Lower Germany was determined to stop this small-scale butchery before it got out of hand: let it pass, and how long would it be before the raiders began slipping across the Rhine itself? Anyway, an object lesson would do the tribes good. This frontier would advance one day soon. The Eagles would cross it in force, and take the eastern bank into the Empire, just as they had already done down south; it was only a matter of time. Eternal Rome could not sit shivering forever before the ghosts of Varus' massacred legions, cold bones these 85 years.

The Prefect of the Noricum Horse had been ordered to send detachments across from the regiment's fort at Dormagen for a week at a time, at each turn of the moon. A thin net of scouts and signallers had been strung along the mouths of the glens; and tonight the net had quivered. A farm had been raided far out on the valley floor; a single appalled survivor had escaped, and blundered on a foundering horse into one of the Roman patrols. Now Flavius Pudens' troop had a good chance of catching the war-party before they could regain the sheltering hills.

Jolting in his saddle in the fourth rank of the troop, Titus Flavius Bassus could not work up much excitement over the prospect of running down naked cattle-thieves. He took his mind off present discomforts by sinking into a pleasant daydream of civilian life, free from trumpets and officers. He had completed his full enlistment, last quarter-day. His discharge, and the diploma of Roman citizenship which came with it, could not be many months away now.

Although he felt all the auxiliary soldier's resentment at not qualifying for the discharge bounty given to the citizen infantry of the legions, he reckoned he had done well enough for an illiterate pony-walloper from upland Thrace. His savings were enough to buy him a half-share of his son-in-law's farrier's shop in the

village outside Dormagen fort. His diploma would make his marriage official, and his sons Roman citizens. His eldest would probably enlist next year, in the legion down stream at Neuss — the VI Victrix.

Titus had been born plain Bassa, son of Mucala, in a high alpine valley south of the Haemus Mountains in Thrace. The Hebrus River valleys had bred horses, and fighting riders, since time out of mind. Rome always recruited foreign cavalry; and in AD 69, when Bassa had just turned 20, General Vespasian's army from Judaea and Syria had come marching through on their way to Italy, and the civil war which would make their leader Emperor. Bassa had enlisted in a Thracian light horse unit; and inside six months he was a veteran of the dreadful, moonlit battle of Cremona. Since then, Rome had turned the wild-riding boy in the fox-fur cap into a skilled professional cavalryman — and had used that cavalryman for all he was worth.

Bassa had fought against Civilis' rebel Batavians down around Rhine Mouth; against the terrible Chatti tribesmen of the Middle Rhine gorges, in five years' of grim campaigning; and against the Saturninus mutiny at Mainz. For the last few years his life at Dormagen fort had been routine enough, thanks be to Epona! Now, with discharge and citizen's rights just over the hill, he had taken a Roman name, picking 'Titus Flavius' in compliment to the Emperor Domitian's family. He had never risen beyond troop farrier, since he still could not read or write; but his Latin was good, after all these years. Not long after the Civilis mutiny, Vespasian had started breaking up national auxiliary

units: Bassa had been posted to the 500-strong Noricum Horse, raised in Austria, and had had to learn the *lingua franca* of the Empire fast.

The shrilling trumpet jerked Titus out of day-dreams of the past and future. The troop was turning round the knee of a hill; and there, lit by the rising sun far out on a slope of heathland, were the war-party — a dozen big men, naked apart from their weapons, jogging along beside a knot of cattle. This was going to be easy. . . The troop shook out into two long lines; as they began to trot, someone gave an ironic hunting-call.

Soldier's luck

The next afternoon, as the troop medical orderly eased Titus up on to the examination table in the legionary hospital at Neuss, the Greek surgeon asked him, 'What went wrong?'

'Wish I knew, sir!' Titus was grey-faced with pain, and the deep javelin-wound in his left thigh had stiffened abominably during the endless, jolting ride back. He had fainted half way across Drusus' Bridge; and old 'Bandage-Box', the medical orderly, had pressed the decurion to halt in Neuss so that Titus could be treated by a real doctor.

Somehow, the charge had got mixed up with the cattle and the gorse-bushes. Titus had lined up his man nicely; then something made old Swallow spook and miss footing, and by the time the German had finally gone down for good under Titus' spear and the horse's flailing hooves, the old trooper had a deep, dirty stab in his leg. Claudius Apollinus pursed his lips over it as he cut away the filthy leather breeches.

'This is going to take a deal of cleaning and searching, my old mountain fox. . . I've wine and poppy-juice to take the fire out of the knife — but I think you had better bite on the gag, all the same. . .'

It was dusk by the time they carried Titus away to a ward. 'Bandage-Box' watched the calm-faced Greek officer washing his reeking hands in a bowl of water and vinegar, while orderlies cleared away the soiled cloths and crusted instruments.

'Will he heal, sir?'

'I hope so, soldier — but it's in the hands of Asclepius. . . That was a deep, awkward cut from a filthy old blade; and the point broke off in the bone. I think I got the shards out; but I'm not entirely happy. His age and condition are against him, I'm afraid. . . . Has he had that cough long?'

'Been barking like an old dog all winter, sir. Drives the rest of us stark mad, at night. But with his discharge coming up, and all, we reckoned we'd be free of him soon enough.'

I hope, thought Claudius Apollinus, *that you don't soon have cause to be sorry you said that, soldier. . .*

Lances for Land: Byzantium, AD 600–1100

It is a summer's day in southern Turkey, some time early in the 960s. The Empire of the Caesars, which Bassus died to defend, has itself been dead these 550 years. Ruined by civil war and a collapsing economy, it was finally unable to hold off the weight of the migrating hordes of barbarians from beyond the Rhine and Danube.

Yet here, in what used to be the Roman province of Cilicia, a strong column of horsemen are riding out to war — horsemen who call themselves 'Romans'. And nobody could mistake these men for barbarian raiders or mercenaries. They are clearly soldiers: disciplined, well-armed, properly equipped and trained, and dressed in smart, expensive uniforms. They ride in ordered ranks, in regiments identified by flags and shield-colours. They are campaigning in obedience to the long-term strategy of a powerful central government, headed by a soldier-emperor so subtle, strong and ruthless that his enemies have christened him 'The White Death'. So, who are these formidable cavalry?

They are soldiers of the Byzantine Empire, the successor to the old Eastern Empire of Rome. Long before Roman Western Europe fell into ruin in the early 400s, the Empire had been formally divided into two more or less separate states, West and East: it was simply too big, too diverse, and faced by too many different problems to be administered any longer by a single man in Rome. When Constantine the Great briefly re-united it in the 330s the capital was officially moved from Rome to Constantinople (Byzantium). When the Teutonic masses swarmed across France, Spain, Italy, Austria and North Africa, the Eastern Empire — most of the Balkans, Turkey, and parts of the Middle East — managed to endure. In fact, it endured so successfully that this surviving part of Rome's Empire lasted another thousand years. At the height of its success in the 10th and 11th centuries it was securely guarded — and even expanded — by one of the finest armies in history: an army built around armoured cavalry.

Mobility vs. numbers

Cavalry had played an increasingly important part in Roman warfare since the 3rd century AD. Old Rome's weakness had been its lack of a central reserve of troops who could deal with invaders if they ever succeeded in breaking into the Empire through the defensive frontier zones held by units like the *Ala Noricorum*, strung out in their thin chain of forts. So new types of cavalry were recruited, and formed into a mobile field army.

Fast-moving cavalry could react quickly to any threat, concentrating at the point of danger; so the army did not have to try to stretch its limited resources so as to be strong everywhere at once. Given that they were not fighting trained, disciplined regiments of infantry like old Rome's legions, the new cavalry could also rely upon their 'shock' effect to defeat much larger numbers of enemy warriors. Both these advantages were vital for an army now desperately short of men and money. But cavalry raised and paid for by the government was still a heavy burden, and Rome could not in the end keep large enough cavalry armies in being. In the Byzantine Empire, always ruled by subtler and more open-minded leaders, a new method of raising horsemen was tried from the 7th century onwards, with lasting success.

A small but high-quality force of regular regiments was based at Constantinople under the immediate command of the Emperor. The rest of the Empire was divided into *thema* or military districts, more than 40 of them in all. Each 'theme' had a military governor, with a small staff and a personal command of a few units of regular cavalry. The rest of the force at his command was drawn at need from men who spent most of their lives at home, farming the land.

Each free cavalryman was given a grant of land at government expense, worth 288 gold pieces (equivalent to four pounds' weight of gold). This good-sized holding could pass from father to son. By good management, many increased in size and value, and it was normal for these soldier-farmers to have servants and slaves. Each holding was responsible for providing in wartime one fully equipped rider and horse — either the holder, his son, a servant, or a paid 'proxy'. Arms, armour and horse belonged to the estate, not to the individual man.

At regular intervals, every three or four years, the soldier reported for a full year's army service. For this he was paid the good wage of 18 gold pieces. This was backed up by disablement pensions, widows' compensation, free rations, special bonuses, and a share in any war booty. On campaign each cavalryman had a servant/groom to care for his horse and do the camp chores. Care was taken to see that the horses and equipment were kept up to standard, even down to such details as the proper fit of soldiers' boots!

The first-class cavalry — *kataphractoi* — wore armour of ring-mail or iron scales, and padded fabric. They carried a 12-foot lance and a long sword, plus either a bow and arrows or a quiver of short, weighted javelins. The units were trained in all the skills and manoeuvres of professional cavalry, as they had evolved since the days of Alexander and Hannibal. The basic unit — *bandon* — was a regiment of some 300 men; it was divided into six 50-man troops — *allaghia* — each of which comprised five ten-man sections — *dekarchiai*. Each section had four 'NCOs' and six troopers.

This system had many advantages. From the men doing their year's service, the governor always had a good force of cavalry at his immediate disposal; and all the soldiers were kept up to a good standard of training. In an emergency the governor could call up a much larger force: for the average province, about 3,000 *kataphractoi*, another 3,000 light horsemen, and as many as 20,000 infantry. (The eastern 'themes' alone could put 30,000 cavalry into the field with only a partial call-up of the best-equipped men). When they were called up, the men served willingly — for they were defending their own home region. When they were not needed they lived at home happily and productively, saving the government the expense of paying and feeding them, and the age-old problem of keeping idle soldiers out of mischief. For centuries this clever arrangement kept the Byzantine Empire secure.

The 'thematic system' broke down eventually; but that was the fault of men, not of the system. In times of weak rule and internal unrest, rich provincial land-owners bought up the holdings of the poorer soldier-farmers, thus gathering the wealth and the men to set themselves up as more or less independent local lords with private armies. This aggravated the problems of government authority; and in time, late in the 11th century, it played a major part in a disastrous defeat for the Empire at the hands of the Turks, which crippled the Empire so badly that it never really recovered.

Anatomy of a cavalry charge

Byzantine cavalry had the discipline which made the difference between an unco-ordinated rush by a

Development of armoured cavalry

We know that in the 2nd to 5th centuries AD, Rome fielded units of heavy armoured cavalry; but we have no clear knowledge of their appearance. It is thought that they were of two types, termed *cataphractii* and *clibanarii*; and that they were influenced by two enemy nations in particular: the Sarmatians, and the Parthians and Sassanid Persians who fought the Romans in Mesopotamia. The Sarmatians (**1**) after driving the Scythians from southern Russia, drifted on westwards. In the late 1st and early 2nd centuries they fought the Romans in the Balkans, and after being defeated they were absorbed as Roman auxiliaries.

They wore scale armour, sometimes of iron, but often — as here — of slices of horse hoof. Their heavily armoured horses wore either the same horn protection, or red-lacquered leather. (**2**) is a Sassanid Persian of the 5th/6th centuries; these riders were among Rome's most dangerous enemies from the 4th century onwards. The 10th century Byzantine *klibanophoros* (**3**) owed something to both these influences. He wore ring-mail, scale, and padded fabric armour, and his horse was protected by hardened oxhide scales. Iron 'splints' and shoes covered his limbs and feet.

mounted mob, and a controlled charge. The shock effect has always depended on a line of riders hitting the enemy together. It took long training for men and horses to learn how to keep their ranks straight and tight as they advanced. Effective charges began at walking pace, only speeding up in the final moments. While outside the killing range of enemy weapons, speed only made it harder to control excited men and horses — and before the invention of powered vehicles, a cavalry charge was about the most exciting wartime experience a man could have.

Ideally, the riders only threw their hands forward, loosed the reins, and kicked their mounts into a gallop in the last 50 or 60 yards. Smashing right through, or into the mass of, the enemy infantry with tremendous impact, each man struck down at the enemy within reach. At this most vulnerable moment they were isolated behind or among the enemy, momentum lost, and ranks inevitably broken up. It was vital for each trooper to spur clear, rallying on trumpets and standards so as to be able to form up and charge on, or back through the enemy, in some kind of order. Obviously, the danger was less if successive waves of cavalry hit the enemy one after another at brief intervals, preventing them from concentrating on one at a time.

The Emperor's Hammer

Below, three Byzantine cavalry *banda* are drawn up for a charge. Good cavalry generals have always ordered several waves of riders to attack one after the other, well spaced out, to break the increasingly weak and disordered enemy by successive hammer-blows. Waves could be separated by hundreds of yards; riders can cover 200 yards in half a minute with ease. Ideally, the second wave only walks forward as the first charges: it is vital to keep the second wave under rigid control, and not to let it get 'sucked in' after the first by the madness of the moment, and the momentum of the charge. The later the riders clap spurs and leap into the final gallop, the better their formation as they hit the enemy.

Here the front unit is one of super-heavy *klibanophoroi*: 384 men forming a wedge 20 men wide at the front, 10 ranks deep and 56 men wide at the rear. About 80 men in two ranks have bows instead of lances.

After this heavy wedge has broken a gap in the enemy front line, other waves of *kataphractoi* will charge in to exploit the advantage. These are the first-class 'thematic' cavalry, lighter and more agile but also armed with a mixture of lances and bows. Earlier Byzantine riders each carried both, using whichever was best in any given situation. Archery declined when Byzantium began to employ Asian mercenary horse-archers; but the 10th-century ruler Leo VI brought bows back for part of each *bandon*, giving the unit this useful, flexible mix of possible tactics once more.

In each 10-man section (enlarged detail) the four NCOs ride at the front and rear of each five-man file. They and the front two troopers have lances, and the third and fourth men have bows.

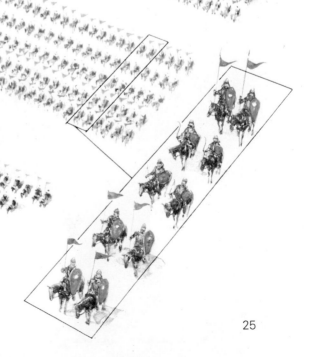

Lances for Power: The Franks, AD 700–1000

A Frankish cavalryman of the 8th-century *scara* — the king's regular troops. When weak kings inherited his throne, Charlemagne's great Frankish empire quickly split up.

While the surviving successors to Rome's Eastern Empire were holding their borders with cavalry armies raised in this imaginative way, a much cruder process was putting men into saddles, and armour on to backs, in the far North-West. Although the ruin of the Western Empire was ruled not by survivors of Roman power, but by its destroyers, they faced exactly the same problems: they needed the mobile weight of cavalry to defend them, yet they lacked resources to pay for it. The Western solution was a system which, at its best, resembled the Byzantine system at its degenerated worst. It produced cavalry without emptying the rulers' coffers; unfortunately, it gradually robbed them of the power to rule at all.

The nightmare of indiscriminate killing and destruction following the collapse of Roman Western Europe early in the 5th century did not last forever. After a generation or two the migrating Germanic tribes settled down among the older inhabitants under the moderately peaceful rule of petty kings. The vigorous barbarian and the educated Romanised Gaul had things to teach each other; slowly they melted together, into a new sort of European — the 'Frank'.

The little, local kingdoms at first had far too few men to spare from the plough, and far too little money, to be able to pay full-time soldiers. Tribal kings had their bands of sworn sword-brothers, whom they supported from the proceeds of petty warfare. In more general emergencies, all able-bodied men were expected to pull their spears from the thatch, and rally to defend king and hearth. There was no discipline beyond individual loyalty, no pay beyond the hope of booty, and none of the training and organisation which turns warriors into soldiers. But from their ex-Roman subjects, the Franks did learn about cavalry.

Most of the barbarian immigrants had been strictly foot-fighters; but now they occupied one of Rome's traditional recruiting grounds for horsemen. And as their kingdoms settled into peaceful age, and began to grow together into a single Frankish nation under a series of strong, far-sighted kings, so they had to face outside challenges more serious than local raiding. Guarding long frontiers demanded the mobility of cavalry.

In the 7th century the birth of Islam sent out shockwaves; and one of them, edged with steel, washed up into the Pyrenees inside a hundred years. From the eastern steppes of their ancestors, the Franks were now faced by a new wave of invaders — the Avars and Magyars — and like the Muslims, these too came on horseback. In the 9th century every foggy estuary began to creep with Viking landing-parties, whose ships gave them all the surprise and mobility of horsemen. The kings who began to consolidate Frankish power under a single throne — Charles 'the Hammer' Martel, Pepin, the mighty Charlemagne, Louis the Pious — all of them needed armoured horsemen to meet these threats. Their treasuries were tiny, by ancient standards; and this was an age when one horse and one set of armour cost 45 *sous* — as much as 20 cows, the whole wealth of a village. The only solution was to parcel out the cost.

Charles Martel is credited with sowing the seeds of the 'feudal system', the pattern of European life for the next 700 years. It amounted to a bargain between a king and his richest subjects. The king was held to own all land. He granted estates to his nobles, in return for sworn support. From the wealth of their estates they would pay a portion in taxes; and they would provide the king with agreed numbers of cavalry for his wars.

By the time Charlemagne, crowned an emperor in AD 800, had stretched the Frankish borders from the Pyrenees to the Prussian forests, this system was producing fine soldiers. We do not know exactly how they fought: they certainly rode to war, but may have dismounted to fight as often as not. The law demanded that they report for duty each with a helmet, body-armour, shield, spear and sword; in terms of equipment they were the equal to their Byzantine contemporaries. They had begun to use stirrups, copied from the Avars, and high-framed saddles; both gave them a more secure seat, allowing more effective use of weapons. Horses — often, now, a sturdy North African 'barb' brought up through Muslim Spain — were shod with iron, giving greater endurance. Though tactics were primitive by Byzantine standards, there was some training, some care for supplies and reconnaissance, some discipline. This could begin to believe itself an 'army'.

The great drawback was that all but a small royal guard owed their obedience not to any king, but to the provincial lords who raised them. And the greedy, self-seeking disunity of the local horse-lords of early medieval Europe would keep armies, and countries, small, weak, and easily beaten for centuries to come.

Sir Fulk Trencavel, 1191

Fulk was already in a sullen temper; when his sergeant pointed out the little knot of riders sitting in their saddles with insolent ease only two hundred paces away, he bellowed with rage.

'*Paynims*?! Here, inside our patrols? Unmolested? God's Wounds!'

Sancho, the Navarrese mercenary who led the ten lightly-armoured cavalrymen sent to escort the water-cart under Sir Fulk's command, made no move from his slouching seat at the lip of the well.

'They slip in and out like smoke, sir knight: it's of no importance. They are only scouts — and Santiago knows, there are no secrets to be hidden in *this* army!'

Knowing that the scarred old sergeant was right only made the 20-year-old Fulk more furiously ready for some outlet for his temper. As the Crusader army marched carefully down the Palestine coast from Acre towards Jerusalem, the Saracens had kept pace through the hills inland. They had swooped down whenever they thought they could tempt the Europeans into breaking formation, but without success. The army was like a great, moving fortress; King Richard of England had strictly forbidden any knight or squadron to break from the protection of the flanking infantry without his express order, signalled by six trumpet-calls.

This had not been what Fulk expected when he had left his father's small manor in the Pays d'Oc last winter, to take the Cross. He had pictured himself charging down the worshippers of Mahound, winning both a Heavenly reward and — of more immediate concern — lands of his own in the Kingdom of Jerusalem. To be *protected* by foot soldiers, forsooth!

There had been a rabble of crossbowmen lounging around this very well when Fulk had ridden up, an hour past. As the only knight present, he had borne himself with the pride proper to a kinsman (albeit a very distant and impoverished kinsman's younger son) of the Viscount of Béziers and Carcassonne. The base-born dogs had straggled out of his way at last, but not without insolence. One bald-headed, pockmarked old ruffian with pale eyes had shouted something in some guttural gabble, and Fulk caught his own sergeants grinning at one another sidelong. These *poulains* he had been given to command were mostly half-castes, their descendants of Syrian Christian mothers and an earlier generation of Crusaders. They seemed to have a smattering of half the tongues in the

28

world; to say nothing of an irksome, independent air. God's Nails! After the disaster of Hattin, four years back, Fulk would not have thought these local-born fighting men had any great claim to put on airs!

His squadron commander was another of these knights who had been rotting out here for years, tainted with Eastern ways. While it was true that Fulk, just three months off the ship from Messina, was still a rather junior knight in the service of the Regent Raymond of Tripoli, still it seemed to him that Sir Lodovic was quite unaccountably unwilling to listen to advice from a fresh viewpoint.

If he was not given a proper opportunity to distinguish himself, how was he to make a reputation, and win land? And like all the younger sons of the Norman world, cast adrift with nothing but a heavy sword and a light purse, Fulk hungered for land — the key to a knight's proper place in the scheme of things.

His smouldering resentment was not soothed by a temperature of 100° in the scanty shade. The August sun beat down on his steel-clad head like a sledgehammer. He was as strong as a young bull, and raised to war from a boy; but he was wearing nearly 50 lbs weight of iron ring-mail over thickly padded undergarments, and his red face streamed with sweat.

As he grabbed the reins of his Flemish stallion from a startled sergeant, he was uneasily aware that his mount was not in the best condition, either. Bought forage was ruinously expensive, and Fulk's purse did not run to as much grain feed as it should: the poor stuff he could afford, mostly chopped straw, blew the stallion out without giving much nourishment. But there was nothing wrong with the stallion's spirit. It shied and plunged as he dragged on the reins, and tried to bite his elbow. He cuffed it into obedience with his fist, and clambered into the saddle.

'No, sir knight! It's not worth it! *'Ware ambush!'*

But Fulk ignored Sancho's alarmed shout, and kicked the stallion into a run. As he thundered towards the dark-faced riders, he thrilled to the smooth power of the muscles beneath him. The Flemish stallion had worked up to a full gallop by the time the knight crashed like a thunderbolt into the group of Saracens with a ringing shout of *'Trencavel!'* Astonished, they were slow to scatter; and one of them fatally misjudged his speed and angle.

Fulk kicked the stallion straight into the shoulder of the silk-clad rider's lighter horse. It reared and screamed, sidestepping as it struggled for balance — and Fulk's broadsword came round in a glittering backhand sweep, shearing through cane shield, arm and ribs, and tumbling the rider out of his saddle like a bundle of bloody rags. With another triumphant bellow, Fulk dragged on the reins, trying to turn the stallion. As the big horse fought the bit, Fulk caught a flash of colour in the corner of his eye.

The Normans were fourth-generation Viking settlers who adapted to the Frankish cavalry tradition. This potent mixture was not a subtle fighter, more a kind of human steamroller: strong, brave, ruthless and tireless. In their hunger for land the Normans spread far afield. The Bayeux Tapestry shows them shipping war-horses to England, where their cavalry won the day at Hastings in 1066.

A hawk-faced rider, guiding a beautiful little grey mare by touches of the knees alone, came dancing up out of the dust on Fulk's blind side, an arrow drawn back to his ear. The stallion plunged heavily round; but the little mare carried its rider out of reach of Fulk's hasty sword-stroke with the agility of a cat, and the bow hummed close beside him. The stallion coughed — stumbled — and died, before Fulk even knew that an arrow had found its heart. It crashed to the ground, sending the knight hurtling over its neck to hit the hard-packed dirt with sickening force.

Fifty paces away, Ibn-Kel, Leader of Ten in the Caliph's *askaris*, gentled his mare Moondove to a halt. He rubbed her ears and crooned to her, and she whickered in pleasure. *'There, there, Drinker of the Wind. . .There, my Dove, my Daughter. . .'* She shared his tent every night, and ate barley from his hand; for was it not written that an angel came down to each horse by night, and kissed its forelock? Now he nudged her gently with one soft-booted toe, and she trotted forward obediently.

Fulk, on his knees in the dust, dizzy and sick with the pain of his broken arm, saw her coming: neck and tail proudly arched, dark forelock bouncing over her little concave face, forelegs slim as blades twinkling in the dust. He stared up dully as Ibn-Kel drew his razor-sharp sword, still crooning to his mare:

'There, my Honey-love, my Swift Arrow. . . Let us finish this blind thing that rushes on its death — and then we shall find you cool streams, and a shade-tree. . .'

'Like Demons Loosed
from Tartarus. . .'
The Mongols,
1200–1300

The 'feudal system', which organised property and power in a pyramid of interlocking obligations, had its heart in those European countries where the Normans settled, or were locally imitated. The Franks had become weak partly because when a land-holder died his estate was split among his sons, breaking up the power-base he had built. The Normans ordered things differently: only the eldest inherited. This loosed upon the medieval world a lawless, warlike breed of younger sons eager to carve out holdings for themselves. They spread across southern Europe and the Middle East; and with them they took their way of warfare, based upon the shock-power of the armoured horseman. They had little interest in footsoldiers. They hired them at need, to occupy the ground won by the cavalry, and to garrison the castles which the horsemen built as border strongholds.

Greedy, proud and quarrelsome, these early 'knights' pursued their private ambitions. They acknowledged few loyalties beyond their oath to the lord immediately above them in the chain of land-holding. Since they were often chronically untrustworthy and restless, Europe was torn by constant warfare, and unable to unite in the face of any new danger which might appear. That danger was born in the late 1160s when, somewhere on the open steppes of Asia, a little boy named Temujin took his first toddling steps beside a nomad campfire. History would remember him as Genghiz Khan; grown to manhood, he became one of the three or four greatest generals of all time.

No armies in history have ever won so many battles or conquered so much territory, so fast, as the Mongol hordes which he raised and trained. The flood of riders which burst from the steppes in the first years of the 13th century defeated every nation in their path. They conquered Russia, in just four years; China; the whole of central Asia; Burma and Vietnam; northern India, and Persia; Syria, and Palestine to the borders of Egypt. They reached the Danube and the Alpine passes of northern Italy; and the fall of western Europe was only averted by their deliberate choice to turn back. These invincible horse-archers out of the East butchered and burned everything in their path: no one will ever know how many millions perished in the shadow of their horse-tail standards.

For a century their ruthless energy dominated and ravaged their world — and then, as suddenly as they had come, they began to drift homewards. The dynasties they had set up to rule Asia slowly withered; but the memory of them has not faded from the

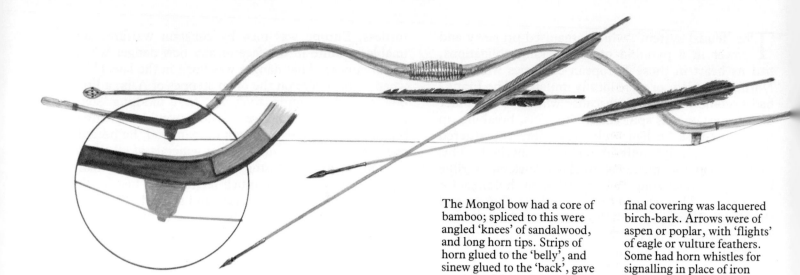

The Mongol bow had a core of bamboo; spliced to this were angled 'knees' of sandalwood, and long horn tips. Strips of horn glued to the 'belly', and sinew glued to the 'back', gave great elasticity and power. The final covering was lacquered birch-bark. Arrows were of aspen or poplar, with 'flights' of eagle or vulture feathers. Some had horn whistles for signalling in place of iron heads.

legends of Europe to this day. They are remembered in the writings of the time as a force more supernatural than human — as 'demons loosed from Tartarus'. Yet their success was based upon simple military excellence, unmatched by any other cavalry army in history.

The perfect campaign cavalryman

It is often thought that the Mongol hordes won their victories by sheer weight of numbers: but it is a lie. They themselves were often outnumbered — they were simply better soldiers than their victims. In discipline, tactical skills, 'intelligence work' and communications the armies led by Genghiz Khan, his son, grandsons, and *orlok* generals were centuries ahead of the 'civilised' West.

The foundation of their success was the Mongol rider and his pony. A nomad of the harsh steppes, bred to the saddle and to self-sufficient survival from his earliest childhood, the Mongol was a brilliant campaign cavalryman while still in his teens. He could ride 80 miles in 24 hours without rest, eating and sleeping in the saddle, and changing from one to another of his string of up to ten spare ponies as each one tired. He ate horsemeat, and drank the milk of his mare. He could stand parching heat, icy cold, and exhaustion better than any Caucasian. His discipline was absolute: the Khan's word was life or death.

Each Mongol tribe was expected to answer the summons to war with almost its entire able-bodied strength between the ages of 14 and 60. They were organised into squads of ten, companies of 100, regiments of 1,000 and divisions of 10,000, each led by officers responsible to the next highest commander — and the senior officers were personally selected by the Khan, and answerable to him. Manoeuvres and tactics were practised in peacetime until they were perfect.

The pony was raised as harshly as the rider: those which survived their training by ordeals of cold, heat, heavy loading, starvation and exhaustion to reach the age of seven or eight were probably as nearly unkillable as any cavalry mount in history. They were small — 12 to 13 hands — and not very fast; but they had astonishing endurance. They ate only grass, so no problems of forage distracted the Mongol commander on campaign. In winter they were left to shift for themselves, 'drinking' snow and surviving as best they could on what greenery they could find beneath it.

The Khan's war-machine

The Mongols followed the sound rule: 'march divided, fight united'. After planning based upon the reports of planted spies, the Khan would send three or four *tumens* — divisions of 10,000 riders — across his borders at widely separated points. This kept the defenders confused as to the route of the main thrust, and avoided competition between the divisions for forage. Each commander had his own orders from the Khan. More important, each was kept in contact with the Khan and with the other divisions by relays of fast message-riders. No other army before the invention of radios was so well co-ordinated.

The defending knights — much less disciplined, much slower to assemble, and much slower on the march — would attempt to meet what they thought was the main attack. They were probably unaware of the other Mongol columns, spreading out each side of them like claws. While the Europeans were ignorant of how many attackers they faced, and from which directions, the Mongol *orloks* were kept closely informed of the knights' movements by spies, advanced patrols, and the Khan's messengers. They could bring other divisions looping in from the sides or rear to envelop the enemy from all sides. The result was usually a massacre.

The prospect of a pitched battle was not allowed to distract the *orloks* from the overall plan of campaign: the Khan was a true strategist. While some divisions were sent to cut off and destroy enemy mobile forces, others would slash deeper and deeper into the enemy rear. They destroyed towns and crops; cut off the enemy king from news, or reinforcements; and drove thousands of refugees, frantic at tales of Mongol savagery, to take shelter in the walled cities. These extra mouths made the task of defending the cities harder, and spread panic among the garrisons.

While cavalry armies are notoriously ill-suited for seige warfare, the Mongols overcame this early problem by pressing into their service — at sword-point — captured Chinese engineers. These specialists devised catapults which could be broken down into packhorse-loads and carried with the army. Cities usually surrendered quickly, and avoided heavy butchery. If they resisted, then their eventual fall meant the massacre of every living thing within the walls. The lesson was quickly learned.

The Mongol armies which pursued this medieval 'blitzkrieg' warfare included both light and heavy cavalry. About two riders in three seem to have been lightly-equipped horse-archers of the classic Asian type. Dressed in layered clothing of felt, silk and leather topped off with the famous Mongol cap with long ear-flaps, they were armed with a powerful bow capable of killing at 200 yards and of penetrating most armour at short range. Each man also carried a sabre or an axe for hand-to-hand fighting; and there are accounts of the use of lariats to entangle and pull down enemies in battle. Some carried javelins, for a heavier close-range 'barrage' of missiles.

The heavier type seem to have been protected by iron or hardened leather helmets; and by suits of armour made of laced strips of iron or lacquered leather. Their ponies were sometimes armoured in this way, too. The heavy cavalrymen also carried the bow, but were armed with a lance as well, fitted with a hook below the head, to pull enemies out of the saddle.

The light and heavy riders were certainly trained to fight together, controlled by the signals of flags, lanterns, fire-arrows, whistling arrows and drums. The armoured men would press home their charge into enemy ranks thinned and weakened by hit-and-run attacks from the light archers. The light troops would follow the heavy into the gap smashed in the enemy line, while others fanned out on the flanks to surround them. When the enemy gave ground — as they almost always did — the light archers would pursue and harry them. Often their retreat was carefully channelled along a route which led straight into a prepared ambush. Against such sophisticated skills, the brave, strong, unimaginitive knights of 13th-century Europe had little chance of victory.

Mongol campaign tactics

In this imaginary example, three divisions advance into an eastern European country by separate routes. Alerted by scouts, two of them converge to encircle and destroy the first force A sent against them by defending border troops. Then one division advances through the main pass in the mountains, confronting and holding the attention of the main defending army B sent out from the city. Meanwhile the other two divisions hook wide around the flanks, riding fast and secretly over routes thought impassible by the Europeans. They swing inwards and divide: part of their strength takes the defenders' army from the flank and rear, and part attacks the city, causing panic and cutting the defending army off from reinforcement or retreat.

These campaigns display all the essential elements of the 'blitzkrieg' tank attacks of the early 1940s, 700 years after the death of Genghiz Khan.

Jean, Lord of Boisvert and Montfaucon, 1356

On a golden September day, in the full pride of his youth and strength, Jean de Boisvert is riding into battle. Ahead of him is the banner, striped *gules et vaire*, of his liege lord Raoul de Coucy, Lord of Montmirail. Around him, careering across a stubble-field in a race to be the first to trade blows with the hated enemy, are a dozen other knights and a score of their squires and retainers. Brave with all the colours of heraldry, glittering in their burnished armour, the chivalry of France tumble across the dun-coloured field like a handful of spilled jewels.

For days now the huge, straggling army of King Jean the Good has been moving south-west to cut off a column of English and Gascons from their retreat into Aquitaine. This time the accursed Black Prince has made one too many raids into France's pillaged heart. Here, at last, a few miles from Poitiers on the northern edge of England's province of Aquitaine, the English and their Gascon jackals will be forced to stand and fight face to face, as knights should fight. After more than ten years of war, the nobility of France are confidently savouring the smell of revenge: revenge for years of meddling in French quarrels, for massacred villages and looted towns, for ruined fields and butchered peasants. Revenge, above all, for the shameful defeat at Crécy ten years before.

Jean de Boisvert is one of a reconnaissance party probing ahead of the main French army. On this hot afternoon of 17 September 1356 they have run into a force of Anglo-Gascon troops here at the farm of La Chaboterie. Their commander, Raoul de Coucy, leads his knights from Boisvert and Offémont, Aunoy and Havraincourt in an immediate, thundering charge — and outrides them all, in his fiery eagerness to get to lance's length with the hated 'Goddamns'. He is no more eager than Jean de Boisvert.

A lord of war

Blazing with the excitement of battle, the 23-year-old Lord of Boisvert and Montfaucon is a splendid figure of a fighting man. He is strong, athletic, a magnificent rider, and completely fearless. As lord of broad estates in Picardy, estates which bring him annual revenues, rents, taxes and tolls of nearly 1,000 *livres*, he is superbly equipped for war. His armour of polished steel plate, worn over padded clothes strengthened with ring-mail, weighs nearly 60 lbs; but it is exactly fitted to his body, and he has been trained to wear it all his adolescent life — he can fight for an hour at a time before its weight and heat seriously weaken him. His

high-framed saddle and long stirrups support him almost in a standing position, braced for the impact of his 18-foot lance in an enemy's steel-clad body, and for the scything blows of broadsword and mace which will follow at hand-to-hand range. His *jupon* and shield are brightly blazoned with the arms of his *seigneurie*.

The stallion that he rides into battle is as awesome as its rider. Bred from Flemish and Lombard stock, and never ridden except to war, it stands a full 17 hands high. It is deep in the barrel, short-coupled, with the great Roman-nosed, 'cold-blooded' head of its kind. Jean calls it 'Tonnerre'; and the earth does indeed seem to thunder as the *destrier's* feathered legs drive iron-shod hooves the size of plates across the churned field of La Chaboterie.

Jean's armour and weapons cost nearly 50 *livres*, and his war-horse another 80: in all, 130 pounds weight of pure silver — at the notional rate for a hired peasant, the equivalent of a field-hand's wages for about one hundred years. But since warfare is the main concern of a nobleman, and since his estates bring him that much in revenues in about six weeks, Jean de Boisvert is unconcerned by the cost.

Jean was born in 1333, the eldest son of a minor aristocrat. The castle of Boisvert is not very much more than a fortified manorhouse, though dominated by the stone-built keep raised by a 12th-century ancestor. It is held in feudal tenancy from the great de

Coucy family, one of the half-dozen most powerful dynasties in France. Through a long saga of war, inheritance, treachery and marriage-alliance the de Coucy barony has grown to embrace more than a dozen different titles and estates. Fertile grain-lands, vineyards, timber plantations, and productive commercial revenues bring in more than 6,000 *livres* annually; and the de Coucys have an obligation to provide the king with more than 30 knights in time of need — one of them, the Lord of Boisvert.

In the terrible pestilence of 1348–50, Jean was orphaned — and so was the 15-year-old daughter of a neighbouring lord. The wisely calculated marriage with Blanche de Montfaucon brought Jean, at the age of 17, a greatly enlarged holding and three vassal knights of his own. He defended his lands with courage, will and pride during that terrible period of anarchy and misery. Since the plague passed Blanche has born her lord four children, of whom two sons survived infancy. Jean de Boisvert can be cautiously optimistic that one, at least, will grow up to carry his shield, with the arms of Boisvert and Montfaucon.

The Knight's world

When he reaches his seventh birthday, Jean's eldest son will leave his mother, and will be sent to the castle of a neighbouring kinsman as a page. In return for his service he will be given the education proper to a nobleman. Blanche will have schooled him in his letters; now he will learn to ride, to hawk, to play chess, to sing and to dance. At 14 he will be made a squire, and while serving his knight he will be taught the skills of war. In his late teens, if he is judged ready for the belt and spurs, he will be knighted himself by his liege lord, de Coucy. He will take his place, ready to follow his father as lord of the family lands. He will have joined the 200,000 members of the noble class — perhaps one per cent of the population of France — in whom all power resides.

The main purpose of Jean's life is war. The bearing of arms and the ruling of inherited lands is what sets him apart from merchants, farmers, and all other despised commoners — and sets him, an obscure country knight, alongside the great dukes of the blood. In theory it is the knight alone — the 'terrible worm in the iron cocoon' — who exposes his body and his property to the danger of war. In return, he enjoys enormous privileges. He is exempt from most taxes; and in his own domain he is the only law, with power over life and death.

In sober fact, the bodies and property exposed to war are usually those of the helpless classes he is supposed to protect. Touchy, impulsive, and with no other real occupation, Jean de Boisvert and his fellows are constantly fighting one another. Since the usual method of waging war is to ravage the lands of the

enemy, the life of the peasant is grim indeed.

In theory, Jean subscribes to the code of chivalry: the obligation of the strong to protect the weak. He believes absolutely in Heaven and Hell, and in his rare moments of self-doubt he no doubt realises that he is a sinful man — violent, hot-tempered, cruel and lustful. But he has been raised to believe that the payment of certain cash sums to the church, and the arrangement of certain rituals, will buy him off divine punishment. Since both God's law and man's bear very lightly on his conscience, he is inclined to be spectacularly wilful — particularly in time of war.

Jean de Boisvert is judged by his fellows in terms of personal prowess in battle. He believes that it is better to die splendidly than to survive defeat. The armies of the 14th century have no real 'command structure': once they are brought to the field of battle, any hope that the knights will obey a tactical plan is vain. Jostling for a chance to win personal glory, Jean is impatient of all authority. He regards detailed planning as faintly cowardly, akin to the vulgar calculation of the merchant's counting-house.

War is the business of noblemen; and France has no properly organised, trained infantry. Footsoldiers are little more than menial servants, useful during boring sieges but of no consequence on the open battlefield. Despised for being useless, they are in fact useless only because they are despised. The English have learned this lesson; and Jean hates them for it. How dare they bring common peasants on to the field of glory, armed with coward's weapons which kill at a distance? Where is the honour in that? The business of war is to fight ones social equals face to face, and beat them by strength and courage.

Unfortunately for class solidarity, the marauding English Plantagenet kings would rather display a proper knightly prowess while winning battles than while losing them. Smaller and poorer than the French, the English aristocracy has grasped that

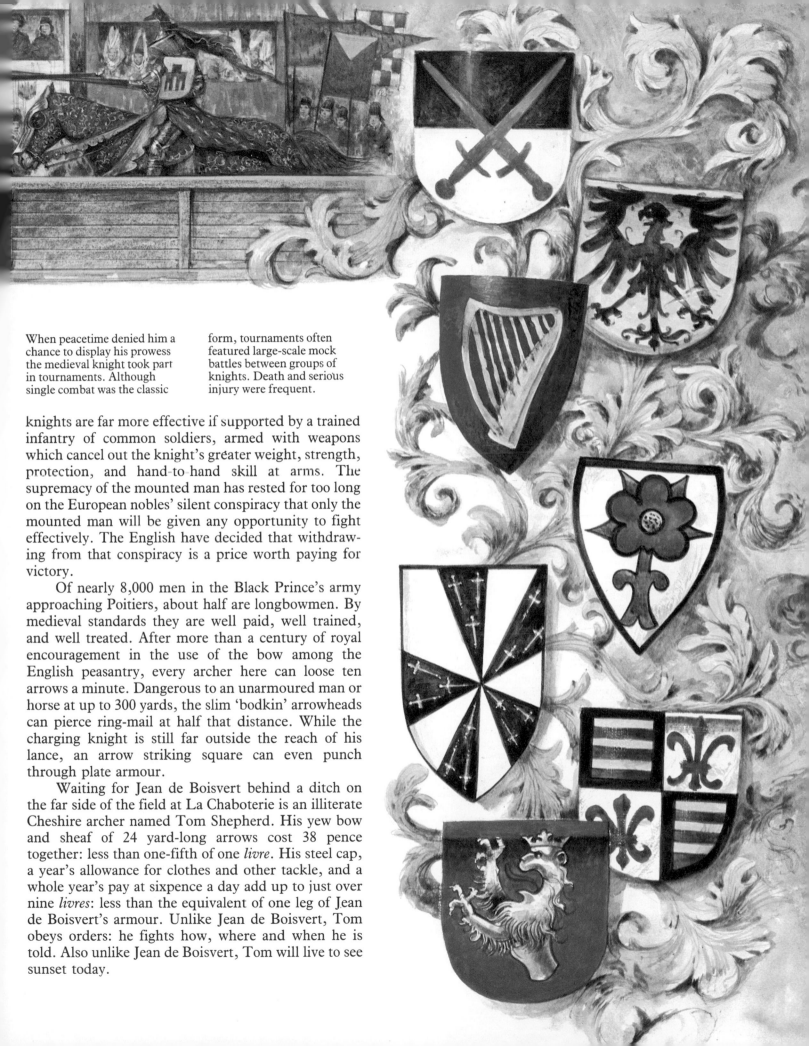

When peacetime denied him a chance to display his prowess the medieval knight took part in tournaments. Although single combat was the classic form, tournaments often featured large-scale mock battles between groups of knights. Death and serious injury were frequent.

knights are far more effective if supported by a trained infantry of common soldiers, armed with weapons which cancel out the knight's greater weight, strength, protection, and hand-to-hand skill at arms. The supremacy of the mounted man has rested for too long on the European nobles' silent conspiracy that only the mounted man will be given any opportunity to fight effectively. The English have decided that withdrawing from that conspiracy is a price worth paying for victory.

Of nearly 8,000 men in the Black Prince's army approaching Poitiers, about half are longbowmen. By medieval standards they are well paid, well trained, and well treated. After more than a century of royal encouragement in the use of the bow among the English peasantry, every archer here can loose ten arrows a minute. Dangerous to an unarmoured man or horse at up to 300 yards, the slim 'bodkin' arrowheads can pierce ring-mail at half that distance. While the charging knight is still far outside the reach of his lance, an arrow striking square can even punch through plate armour.

Waiting for Jean de Boisvert behind a ditch on the far side of the field at La Chaboterie is an illiterate Cheshire archer named Tom Shepherd. His yew bow and sheaf of 24 yard-long arrows cost 38 pence together: less than one-fifth of one *livre*. His steel cap, a year's allowance for clothes and other tackle, and a whole year's pay at sixpence a day add up to just over nine *livres*: less than the equivalent of one leg of Jean de Boisvert's armour. Unlike Jean de Boisvert, Tom obeys orders: he fights how, where and when he is told. Also unlike Jean de Boisvert, Tom will live to see sunset today.

Fashions in Steel

Throughout the medieval period the knight's armour went through a steady process of improvement. The armourer, practising with new materials and ways of shaping them and fitting them together, tried to give his clients greater protection from enemy weapons. At the same time the fighting man tried to find ways of getting round each improvement in armour, so that he could still reach his enemy's body with his weapons. The development of armour took the form of a steady increase in the use of shaped plates of steel over more and more of the body surface. Beginning with the all-enveloping helmet added to basically ring-mail protection from the early 1200s onwards, it ended with complete suits of perfectly articulated plates in the late 1400s.

Ring-mail was flexible; it could be worn all over a knight's body, and stayed in place however violently he moved. Worn over thick, padded garments to cushion the force of blows from a piercing blade, it gave good protection against hand weapons. But it would not stop the lance of a charging rider, and it would not stop arrows at short range.

From the middle of the 13th century onwards, knights added pieces of steel plate over the top of mail at the most vulnerable points: cup-shaped plates at

Above: Sir John d'Abernoun, c. 1330
Sir John wears armour of what is called the 'cyclas period': after the long gown worn over armour, here in Sir John's heraldic colours — 'Azure, a chevron Or'. The short-cut front gives ease of movement when fighting on foot or mounting a horse. The armour is of several mixed types: ring-mail, plate, and padded and metal-reinforced fabric. Under the gown is the padded, studded *gambeson*. Under this is the mail *hauberk*; and under this another layer of padding, the *haqueton*. Arms, shins, shoulders, elbows and knees are protected by shaped plates laced over the mail. The 'great helm' was now being discarded in favour of the smaller *bascinet*, shaped to send blows glancing off, and laced to the mail *camail* covering the neck.

Right: Italian knight, c. 1385
Apart from mail still visible at the vulnerable shoulder/neck/armpit area, and in a skirt around the loins, plate has almost covered the body by this date. This is the type of armour worn by most knights of the Agincourt period. The helmet is the *'houndskull' bascinet*, named from its long, snouted visor. This is hinged so that it can be raised, and has slits and holes for ventilation and vision. The skull is shaped to a domed point to 'throwoff' blows. The plate breast armour has a skirt of overlapping plates — the *fauld* — which slide over one another like the sections of a lobster's tail if the knight bends over. The limbs are almost entirely protected by fitted plates. The gilded strips around the edges of the plates are simply for decoration: knights loved displaying wealth.

elbow and knee, gutter-shaped plates on the outer surface of arms and legs. Thickly padded fabric, sometimes with mail and small iron plates rivetted inside, was worn both under and over ring-mail in various 'sandwich' arrangements. 'Coats of plates' were worn over mail on the chest and back: these were layers of fabric with small metal scales 'built in', making a fairly flexible 'jacket'. It was only a matter of time before complete breast-plates, and later, complete breast and back-plates, began to appear. By the mid-1300s 'up to date' knights were almost completely covered with plate.

The 15th century saw the armourer's art brought to perfection. He could now fit a knight with a completely articulated suit made up of dozen of plates; if properly measured for the client it was surprisingly easy to move about in, with each plate sliding over the next as a limb flexed. So cunningly made were these armours that shields were unneccesary. The smooth, fluted plates were designed to send weapon blades glancing and skidding off their surface harmlessly. Armour had become so effective that, as one knight wrote, it stopped you getting hurt, and stopped you hurting anyone else. Gunpowder would eventually change that situation dramatically.

Left: Earl of Warwick, c. 1450
This Milanese-made armour, typical of the uncovered, polished 'white' armour of the Wars of the Roses period, is copied from the tomb effigy of Richard Beauchamp, Earl of Warwick, who died in the 1430s. The effigy was made 20 years later, so shows us armour of a style slightly later than the earl's actual lifetime. Exactly measured to the knight's body, this superb piece of engineering hardly hindered normal movement. It weighed about 70 lbs, with the weight so well spread over the body surface that a normally strong and athletic man could run, ride and fight without much difficulty. Old stories of knights having to be lifted into the saddle with a crane are misunderstood: they applied only to special tournament armour. Crests were probably not worn in real battles.

Above: Thomas Saville, c. 1590
This beautifully decorated armour is typical of the period when plate protection no longer offered serious advantages in battle. Aristocrats still spent fortunes on fine armour for tournaments and gala occasions, however. The blueing, etching, gilding and chasing looked magnificent; but decorative features sometimes 'cluttered up' surfaces which should have been left smooth to 'throw off' blows — a sure sign that armour was no longer a serious military necessity. These lavish armours often followed the shape of the fashionable clothes of the period. This example has a torso drawn down into the pointed shape of a doublet, and the hips and thighs balloon out like the puffed breeches of late Elizabethan costume. Gorgeous display was more important than protection by this date.

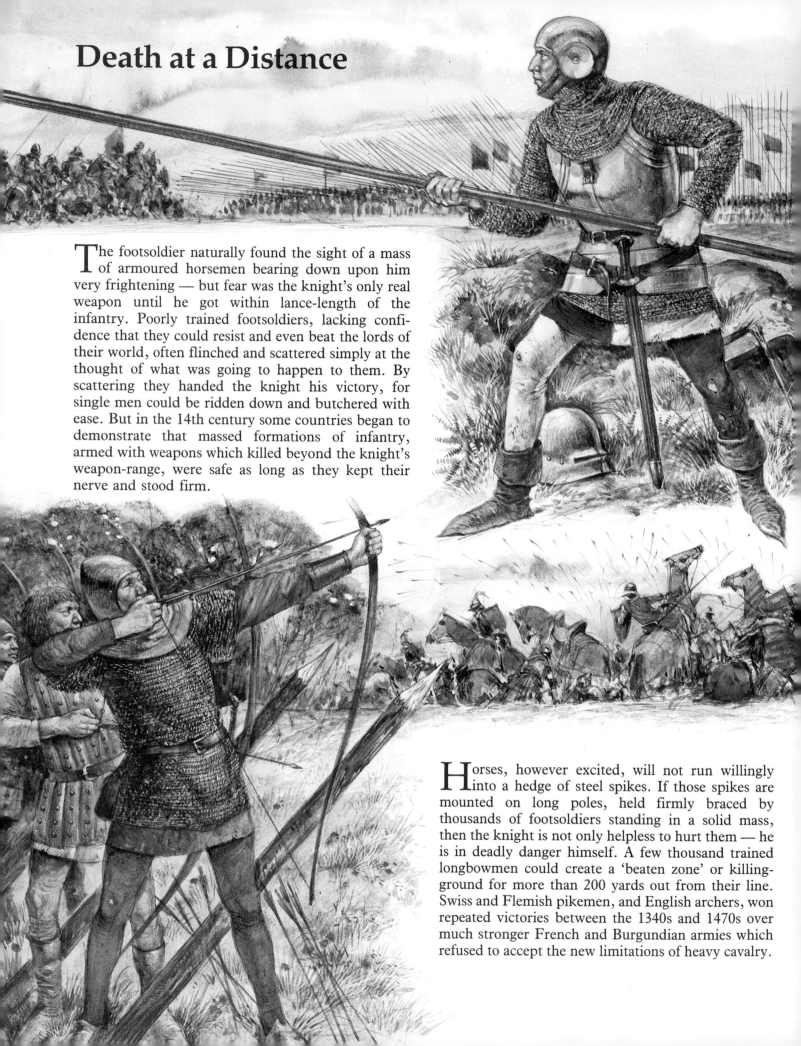

Death at a Distance

The footsoldier naturally found the sight of a mass of armoured horsemen bearing down upon him very frightening — but fear was the knight's only real weapon until he got within lance-length of the infantry. Poorly trained footsoldiers, lacking confidence that they could resist and even beat the lords of their world, often flinched and scattered simply at the thought of what was going to happen to them. By scattering they handed the knight his victory, for single men could be ridden down and butchered with ease. But in the 14th century some countries began to demonstrate that massed formations of infantry, armed with weapons which killed beyond the knight's weapon-range, were safe as long as they kept their nerve and stood firm.

Horses, however excited, will not run willingly into a hedge of steel spikes. If those spikes are mounted on long poles, held firmly braced by thousands of footsoldiers standing in a solid mass, then the knight is not only helpless to hurt them — he is in deadly danger himself. A few thousand trained longbowmen could create a 'beaten zone' or killing-ground for more than 200 yards out from their line. Swiss and Flemish pikemen, and English archers, won repeated victories between the 1340s and 1470s over much stronger French and Burgundian armies which refused to accept the new limitations of heavy cavalry.

Crossbows were thick bowstaves mounted across a wooden stock. At first made of glued layers of horn and wood, they were later forged from sprung steel. Early bows could be loaded by fitting a belt-hook to the string, standing in the 'stirrup', and then straightening up. Later types were so stiff that they needed a mechanical jack or windlass to pull back the string. The short, heavy 'bolts' could punch right through armour and kill men and horses at most practical battle ranges. They did not need much strength or long training before they could be used effectively. The disadvantage was the slow loading — with the mechanical devices it took about half a minute, giving cavalry time to charge home before a second volley could be fired.

The first 14th-century handguns were like miniature cannon mounted on wooden poles, fired by pressing a red-hot wire into gunpowder exposed in the 'touch-hole'. 15th-century types were longer, more accurate, and had mechanical triggers which lowered smouldering cord into the touch-hold. Like crossbows, their great weakness was the slow loading. If gunners were given the protection of pikemen, or entrenched behind a stockade, they could do great damage; used *en masse*, as by the Spaniards at Cerignola in 1503, they could slaughter armoured cavalry, who were unable to reach them.

Pistols and Caracoles, 1500–1620

As we look back on our history, it is tempting to arrange events into neat patterns of cause and effect. With the easy wisdom of hindsight, we assume that the direction events took was inevitable, and must have seemed obvious. But real life is not that tidy; and the people who live through events see only a distorted, local picture, not the broad sweep of a general trend. To us, the introduction and slow improvement of hand-held guns, and the appearance of disciplined infantry to use them, may seem to sound an obvious warning to cavalry that their days were numbered; but that is only because we already know how the story ended.

At the beginning of the 16th century these grimy, roaring battalions lugging their miniature cannon awkwardly around the battlefield were a good deal more confusing. They were confused themselves, in a sense. And it took several generations of steady improvement of their ungainly and unreliable weapons, and of the development of tactics for them by trial and error, before the picture became clear. In the meantime, cavalry still had a very important part to play.

War was still ruled by the nobility; and the attitude of the nobility — both those who faced, and those who made use of the new gundpowder weapons — may be guessed by the titles they bore, and still bear today right across Europe: knight, chevalier, ritter, caballero. . . . The nobleman's place in war was in the saddle of horse. The new guns were a novelty, which might enjoy a fashionable popularity among unscrupulous generals before returning to the obscurity they deserved. They were certainly not fitting weapons for gentlemen. 'Would to heaven', wrote a Frenchman, 'that this accursed engine had never been invented'. It had been the death of many valiant men, 'slain for the most part by the most pitiful fellows and the greatest cowards. . . poltroons that had not dared to look those men in the face . . . which at distance they laid dead with their confounded bullets'.

There were good reasons, apart from class prejudice, to doubt the usefulness of guns in the long term. The early hand-guns were a good deal slower to use than the longbows they replaced; they could not be used in wet weather; and their accurate range was shorter than that of the bow. But men could be taught to use them with much shorter training than the lifelong practice needed by a master archer; and if used *en masse*, by men protected against their particular weaknesses, they were increasingly deadly.

Standard-bearer of an Austrian 'cuirassier' (heavy cavalry) unit, about 1620. Horsemen spent as much time fighting other cavalry as infantry; and since pistols were chancy weapons, and most fighting was done with the sword in a cavalry mêlée, armour was still useful. Thick enough to stop most pistol-balls, it gave no protection against infantry muskets unless made so heavy that it was troublesome to wear. Pistols were quickly 'used up' in battle, as most riders carried only two or three. It was impossible to reload when actually in close combat — writers of the day suggested that riders use their empty pistols as clubs!

Apart from its real usefulness, there was a sentimental reluctance to abandon forever the knightly armour of old.

The main weakness was the slowness of loading, which left hand-gunners vulnerable to a quick cavalry charge before they could fire a second volley. So mixed units of gunners and pikemen became the usual arrangement for infantry, the pikes defending the gunners during reload. These quite complex tactics required discipline, and the training of organised regiments of infantry accustomed to serving together as a body. The emergence of the first paid, professional armies began to parallel the improvements in firearms and tactics during the 16th century.

In 1520, at about the same time that Blaise de Monluc wrote his bitter words about 'poltroons' and their 'confounded bullets', the far-sighted Italian, Machiavelli, was writing of cavalry: 'Do not look upon them as the main force of an army. . . . They are highly necessary to reconnoitre, to scour roads . . . and to lay waste an enemy's country, and to cut off their convoys; but in the field battles which commonly decide the fate of nations, they are fitter to pursue an enemy that is routed and flying than anything else.'

The stately dance of battle

In the mid-1500s cavalry were going through a transition. They were no longer the knights of old, invincible in the charge. They were not yet what they would become — the mounted equivalent of the infantry regiments, trained to play the part in the overall plan of battle for which their particular qualities and weapons suited them. They were, frankly, confused: and they took a way out of that confusion which for generations robbed them of their best remaining advantage — their ability to move fast, and shock an enemy with their impact. Since guns were the coming thing, very well: cavalry would be given guns themselves. The knight became a mounted pistoleer.

This was a bad idea, because 16th-century guns were quite unsuited for effective use on horseback. By this time the first generation of 'matchlock' hand-guns, fired by applying a piece of burning fuze to gunpowder in a small 'priming pan' connected by a hole to the main charge in the barrel, were being replaced by the 'wheellock' type. It was obviously not practical for a horseman to manage his mount while messing about with bits of smouldering string and loose gunpowder: the wheellock seemed to offer a solution. It was fired by a spring-loaded wheel with a roughened edge rotating against a piece of iron pyrites, which threw sparks into the priming powder. It could be loaded, and its mechanism wound up with a small spanner, and then set aside ready for use when needed.

The major problem was that of accuracy. Circus trick-shooters apart, it is almost impossibly difficult for a man on a moving horse to shoot a hand-held gun

with any accuracy — even a modern gun. The short-barreled, smooth-bore wheellock was so inaccurate that its user had to come to a halt if he was to have any chance of hitting his enemy; and even then, he had to come so close that the muzzle was almost touching the target. When Western cavalry largely abandoned the lance in favour of pistols, from about 1540 onward, they had to adopt tactics which robbed them of their shock effect without bringing any real advantage to compensate.

The typical manoeuvre of late 16th-century horsemen was called the 'caracole'. Faced with enemy infantry, a block of horsemen — more of a 'deep column' than the classic 'broad line' of old — would trot forward. One rank at a time, they would advance to within short range, halt, fire their pistols, then swing off to the side and fall back to the rear of the column, allowing the next rank to advance and fire in its turn.

To accomplish this tricky manoeuvre in the din and confusion of battle was obviously very difficult; and one wonders how often more than the first rank or two managed it before casualties, blinding smoke, a panicky horse, or a sudden and unexpected move by the enemy reduced the whole solemn dance to a shambles. The deliberate pace meant that they had to face at least one volley from the longer, steadier, more accurate, and more densely-massed guns of the infantry as they advanced to fire. The halt to fire

meant that even if the infantry facing them showed signs of unsteadiness as a result of the pistol fire, the horsemen had lost all impetus, and could not 'charge home' to exploit the advantage.

The man who rescued the cavalry from this blind alley was one of the greatest generals of all time: Gustavus Adolphus, King of Sweden 1611–1632. His army, which he personally planned and led, was one of the most efficient to fight in the Thirty Years' War. This terrible series of campaigns, between 1618 and 1648, tore apart Germany and the neighbouring territories of central Europe. It was a war of senseless destruction and horrible cruelty, which left large areas devastated by pillage, massacre and plague.

Balanced armies

Gustavus' genius lay in his understanding of the need to co-ordinate the different parts of an army, and in the energy and skill with which he put his ideas into practice. His army was formed and trained to fight in such a way that the different strengths and weaknesses of foot, horse, and artillery meshed together. He increased the firepower of his infantry, and trained them to change formation and direction neatly and calmly even in the thick of battle. He introduced much lighter and more mobile cannon than had previously been used. Instead of being limited to static siege warfare, his artillery was organised and equipped to move about the battlefield quickly, firing in support of

the horse and foot. And he restored to the cavalry the 'shock' effect that had been lost for more than sixty years.

The deep columns disappeared, to be replaced once again by long lines, three ranks deep. The pistol was now to be kept for emergency use once the cavalry had already charged at speed into the enemy ranks — and that charge was to be made sword in hand. What enabled the horseman to charge with a good chance of success was the supporting fire of the foot and guns. Infantry with increasingly efficient muskets, and the new mobile cannon, were sent right forward alongside the cavalry to fire into the close-packed ranks of the enemy infantry. Only when the enemy front had been shaken and broken up by their fire did the cavalry charge home in the traditional way. This change made all the difference.

When cavalry faced enemy cavalry they did not need such close supporting fire, which was anyway not practical against fast-moving targets. The 'caracole' had never been any use against cavalry, and the old sword-against-sword mêlée had remained unchanged except by the introduction of close-up pistol-fire as opportunity offered.

Gustavus' tactics, noted and copied by other nations, were soon to be seen on the fields of England when the Civil Wars between Parliament and the Stuart kings threw up another cavalry leader of genius: Oliver Cromwell.

Right: How the 'caracole' was performed against infantry.

Left: Armies of the 16th–17th centuries included both heavy cuirassiers, and more lightly armoured 'harquebusiers' with wheellock (later, flintlock) carbines. Drill manuals of the day are astonishingly complex. They suggest that troopers and horses were trained to perform what can only be called circus tricks. These included the repeated firing and reloading of muzzle-loading guns while in the saddle, at speed. Under perfect conditions, one can believe that some special demonstration units might have achieved such miracles; that ordinary troopers could perform them regularly in battle is frankly incredible. The introduction of the flintlock made guns cheaper and more reliable, since the moving parts were fewer and stronger; but it made loading no easier.

Corporal Fortitude Whitton of the Captain-General's Horse, 1645

Even at noon the watery April sun gave little heat;
but Fortitude was comfortable enough on his
bench outside the inn, with bread and cheese and ale,
and the fascinated company of the goodwife's children, while he kept half an eye on the smith working
on Crimson's hoof across the way. His gelding had
thrown a shoe during one of the Troop's training
patrols through these damp Thames Valley meadows
around Windsor; and Captain Berry had left his
corporal here in Winkfield, with sixpence for the
smith, and leave to catch up at his leisure. Corporal
Whitton was a steady man, who had fought at James
Berry's shoulder in many a hard fight these last three
years of civil war: the captain was content to give him
an hour of ease.

All spring the countryside around Windsor had
been abustle with the comings and goings of the
Parliament's New Model Army forming and training.
A mighty instrument was being forged for the Lord's
work — a blade pointed at the heart of Charles Stuart,
the Man of Blood, and his hell-raking cavaliers.
Fortitude took pride in his work of training, though it
was easy enough. By far the majority of the troopers of
Fairfax's Horse — the Captain-General's Own — were
veterans of Noll Cromwell's old 'Ironsides', divided
now into two new 600-strong regiments under Sir
Thomas Fairfax himself, and Colonel Whalley. Most
were good, steady men, thought Fortitude: though
Major Desborough had been obliged to speak sharply
about a saddle which that ill-named wight Merit
Topcliffe had *certainly* sold for beer, whatever he said
to the contrary; and Zeal-for-the-Lord Langdyke drew
Chaplain Joshua Sprigge's stern eye by his occasional
zeal for serving-wenches. . . .

Fortitude glanced across at the smithy, where
Crimson's hoof was being cleaned, gripped between
the smith's aproned knees. He was sure that shoe had
been no more than four weeks in place: he would have
words with the farrier when he got back to billets. He
turned back to the children, who had come running to
gawp — from a safe range — at the scarred trooper in
his red coat and dark steel. The lad had been an easy
capture: a grin, and the offer of the big, three-bar
helmet had lured him close. But the little maid, so like
his own Bridget far away in Huntingdon, had demanded a campaign worthy of the siege of Breda to tempt
her any closer to the sinister eyepatch. Fortitude was
on familiar ground, however: he made mice of his
fingers, in and out of his boot-tops, until she fell into
his ambuscado. Once she even climbed to his lap,
though not for long: the steel breastplate made an
indifferent soft pillow for her velvet cheek. The
corporal sighed, and thought again of his home in
St. Ives, and of his wife Goody, and Bridget and little
Miles.

Englishman against Englishman

It had been a long war, and a bloody one, since he had enlisted for Captain Cromwell's Troop that September day in Huntingdon, back in '42. He had cost the Parliament two shillings a day, plus £7–10s.–0 for Crimson; and about £6–0–0 for his back-and-breast, 'pot' helmet, buff coat, boots, sword, pistols and belts. Parliament had cost *him* three years of his prime — and an eye put out by a French cavalier with an old-time rapier outside Gainsborough back in July 1643, the day three Troops of Cromwell's Horse drove Sir Charles Cavendish's men into a bog, and Captain-Lieutenant Berry killed Cavendish himself. Fortitude remembered little of the dreadful retreat to Lincoln the next day: he had been tied in his saddle, his head bound up with somebody's shirt-tail, half out of his mind with pain. He thanked the Lord for his deliverance, nevertheless. If the jerk of his tortured head had not snapped the rapier point between the visor-bars that instant, it would have reached his brain. As it was, it was a miracle he had survived the months of fever during the hungry summer of '43.

Privately, though he had not told even Chaplain Sprigge, he feared his wound was a judgement for his sinful pride and cruelty. There had been a mad evening fight outside Grantham that May, when Noll's troopers slew a hundred Royalists for the loss of two of their own. That night Fortitude had been possessed by the horrible pleasure of riding down fleeing enemies like rabbits; he had laughed and cursed as he leant easy from the saddle to split their defenceless heads with his heavy broadsword, and the blood had thundered in his ears with the sheer, arrogant excitement of the avenging horseman. God was not mocked, and to Him was the victory: Fortitude was shamefully certain that his eye had been required of him in penance for the bloody ride by Grantham. He was no longer the kindly farmer who had left Goody's arms with such high-minded ideas about smiting the Man of Blood for the liberties of honest Englishmen tyran-nised by a high-stomached prince.

The smith's hammer range like a sword on armour: he had taken the cherry-red shoe from fire to anvil, and was making nail-holes with a spike. The din of battle was as familiar now to Corporal Whitton as the gentle sounds of his own kitchen had once been to Farmer Whitton. He might be a harsher man now; he was also incomparably a better soldier. When he had joined Oliver Cromwell's first little band of fifty or sixty Cambridge and Huntingdon yeomen back in '42, he had known nothing of war. Now he was fit to face any cavalryman in the world.

From the first, Cromwell had picked men carefully for his 'lovely company'. He wanted sober, responsible countrymen, not the 'decayed serving-men and tapsters' who straggled along under other Troop standards. He and his officers laboured night and day against a chaotic chain of command, an inadequate system of supply, and simple ignorance. Parliament had many senior officers who had fought in Germany and the Low Countries, but very few veterans at Troop level. Earnest, turnip-faced squires in old-fashioned armour had to learn the first principles of leading cavalry in war, with the mud of their East Anglian acres still caked on their boots, and Cruso's *'Militarie Instructions for the Cavallerie'* open in their hands.

There had been mistakes, and defeats in plenty, before they had learned to get the measure of Prince Rupert's hard-mouthed gentlemen's sons, whose birth gave them the spirit to ride like angels and fight like devils. But in the end, discipline won over arrogant courage: Noll's troopers obeyed their recall trumpets, and Rupert's lordlings would not. Now Noll was Lieutenant-General of the Horse in this New Model Army — with 'Daddy' Skippon of the Foot, Cromwell ranked second only to Sir Thomas Fairfax himself. And this new army would win the war, of that Fortitude was certain. Nothing like it had been seen before: trained, organised, disciplined regiments,

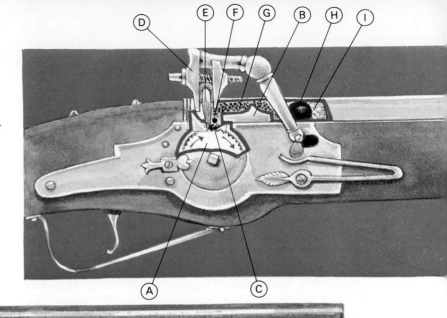

Left: Details are unknown, but Berry's Troop probably charged in three close ranks of about 30 troopers each. Capt. Berry (*orange*) rode, with two trumpeters (*yellow*), at the right of the front rank, which had the best men. The cornet (*red flag*) rode in the centre, the lieutenant (*red*) at the left. These officers were 'covered', behind or on their blind side, by corporals (*blue*). From his place behind the rear rank the quartermaster (*dark green*) could watch the whole unit.

Right: Fortitude's wheellock pistols worked like this: Trigger released notched wheel A held by spring, to spin, and pan cover B to slide forward exposing powder C. Sprung 'cock' D held wedge of pyrites E against notched wheel, making sparks to set off priming powder. Flame went through hole F to main charge G inside barrel, where ball H was held tight by paper wad I. The complex mechanism broke easily, and was tricky to repair.

pledged to serve anywhere in the land for as long as was needful, and led by proven commanders.

New standards

It had been a wrench, at first, to learn that the old 'Ironsides' were to be dispersed. But though his regiment was new, most of his old comrades were still with him — and Captain Berry, who had named him corporal in his new Troop. And he was proud to ride with Fairfax. He had seen the quiet-spoken, gypsy-dark Yorkshireman fight like a man possessed at Winceby back in October of '43 — bare-headed and bloody, at the head of his psalm-singing troopers. He was a wise commander, and a just and godly man, who kept his devil leashed until the day of battle.

Cromwell's Horse had won their name of 'Ironsides' from the mouth of proud Rupert himself, in the terrible fight at Marston Moor in July 1644. Fortitude remembered it like a bad dream: a dank, chill evening when 40,000 Englishmen fought for their beliefs — and more than 5,000 lay dead for them in the pouring rain before darkness fell. The first thunder had cracked the sky open as Cromwell led them forward on the left wing at a controlled trot. They had hit Lord Byron's Royalist cavalry like a stone wall on the move. Fortitude had fired his first pistol point-blank into a man's belly; his second, into another's horse; and then gripped the sword dangling from his wrist-strap, and slashed at the cuirass-fastenings and reins of a third. The cavalier's reins parted, his mount shied, and Fortitude's point took him through the hollow of the throat. The staring white face sank out of sight between the kicking horses like a man drowning in a dark sea.

Fortitude recalled little in detail, after that first kill with the sword. But he knew well enough that the 'Ironsides' had held together under Rupert's furious counter-attack; and regrouped, and charged a second time; and then *again*, right across the rear of the King's army, to tear up Goring's left wing cavalry. *That's* what made soldiers worthy of the Lord of Hosts: the self-command to obey the trumpet, and not to squander all in one mad career over the fields.

The sharp stink of scorched hoof and the sound of hammer and file brought him to his feet at last, and he strolled over to the smithy. The smith straightened up from twisting off the last protruding nail-end with his pincers, and Crimson got his four feet under him again, as quiet as a cat. The old smith patted his neck.

'Good, steady beast, master. . . But do you find a gelding answers — in war, like?'

Fortitude fished under his buff coat, and brought out a golden, wrinkled, winter-stored apple, as sweet as honey. His horse whickered, and butted him softly till he offered it on his palm.

'Answers for *me*, friend. 'Course, there's some fine lords'ld rather die in a ditch than ride ought but a stallion entire — and that's just what they do, oft-times. . . Might serve for hallooing after game; but a stallion's too chancy, in a fight.' He absently ran a hand over Crimson's muzzle, feeling the 'seven-year hooks' growing at the back of his teeth.

'He's carried me faithful these three years, and he's good for plenty yet. . . 'Tis not blood and fire wins a battle, friend; 'tis knowing your duty to the Lord, and obeying the trumpets. . .'

Cuirassiers, Hussars and Dragoons, 1700–1800

By the late years of the 17th century, cavalry tactics had come round in a full circle, and were once again recognisable as those of the ancient world. Cromwell's troopers won battles like Marston Moor by methods which would have been quite understandable to Hannibal 2,000 years before.

From the viewpoint of a bird flying high overhead, an 18th-century army drawn up for battle would not have looked unlike an army of Imperial Roman legionaries and auxiliaries. In the centre the long lines of infantry were drawn up in ordered blocks. The cavalry, in smaller blocks, were placed out on each wing, facing the enemy cavalry. The battle was usually decided by the behaviour of the infantry. The task of the horsemen was to try to sweep the enemy cavalry away, leaving the ends of the long lines of footsoldiers unguarded, and open to attack from more than one direction at once.

Although the cavalryman, fighting in the saddle with sword or lance in hand, had another 150 years of serious importance ahead of him, he had already reached something very like his final method of fighting. The next century and a half would see very little in the way of radical changes of tactics.

In the 18th century, gradually and unevenly, the trooper would be taught to charge further and faster; and the importance of his firearms would decline even more sharply than it had since the days of Gustavus' reforms. In the middle years of the century the greatest European victories were won by the Prussian armies of King Frederick the Great, who placed great importance on his cavalry — though always as a 'partner' to his infantry, and never as the central factor in his battlefield calculations. Frederick demanded

that his cavalry always charge with the sword: pistols and carbines were to be used only for guard duties. He also made sure that his drilled squadrons could charge hundreds of yards at full gallop, in contrast to the 'charge at the trot' typical of Cromwell's battles a hundred years before. The thinking behind this change was Frederick's determination to send his horsemen tearing into the enemy with the greatest possible shock effect.

The picture of those orderly ranks of Prussians, keeping their formation while riding across as much as a mile of open ground, to crash hell-for-leather into the shaken ranks of the enemy, raises two important points. Firstly: how could the 18th-century generals keep a discipline and order so far beyond that achieved even by men like Cromwell; and secondly, why did they think the shock effect of a flat-out run, rather than a controlled trot or canter, so important?

The first answer is that the 18th century saw the return, for the first time since the days of Rome and Byzantium, of the truly professional, full-time, national army. The world was changing, and armies changed like everything else.

The 17th and 18th centuries saw the merchants of the old European countries reaching out across the seas for trade, and bringing back new wealth. This wealth created a new 'middle class' of businessmen and officials, which become far more important than the old landed aristocracy. The merchants wanted order, and strong government; and they were happy to support their monarchs, with taxes and with service, in order to wrest the real power away from the old privileged classes. The wealth they created enabled the monarchs to raise and pay for full-time 'standing' armies; and full-time armies had the time, the money, and the continuity of organisation to turn out soldiers so obedient and well-practised that they could perform complicated drills with precision and regularity.

The second question — the importance of maximum shock in a cavalry charge — has a surprising answer. It was important for cavalry to charge furiously fast, and in unbroken ranks, because this produced the most frightening spectacle for the enemy who were facing the charge. We cannot know exactly what happened in ancient and medieval battles; but the eyewitness accounts of soldiers of the last 250 years are almost unanimous: in a great majority of cases, the enemy had already begun to turn and run *before* the charging cavalry actually hit them. The 'moral effect' of a cavalry charge was actually the most important weapon the horseman had.

If we picture the scene from the point of view of the men being charged, it is not so hard to understand

European heavy cavalry, late 17th to mid-18th centuries:
Left: Polish lancer, 1680s. During centuries of warfare against the Turks on Europe's eastern frontiers, military styles remained rather old-fashioned, and also borrowed features from the Oriental enemy. This rider — one of the troopers of the Polish King John Sobieski's relief force, which saved Vienna from the Turks in 1683 — still wears half-armour. The fantastic wooden and eagle-feather 'wings' fixed to his back-plate are purely decorative. Apart from a lance and flintlock pistols, he also has the medieval combination of a heavy, curved sabre for slashing, and a long, slim sword for stabbing.

Centre: Austrian Cuirassier, c. 1710. A trooper of the 'Marlburian' period, he still wears almost exactly the same outfit as Cpl. Whitton, 60 years before. At the beginning of the 18th century he would still have worn the *zischagge* helmet. Sabre-cuts to the head were still too dangerous for protection to be abandoned altogether, however: under the cocked hat is an iron strapwork protective cap. Since most cavalry-versus- cavalry fights were still decided with the sabre, and would be for 150 years, the heavy trooper's breast-and-back armour lasted well into the 19th century: in the French army, until 1914.

Right: Prussian Cuirassier, 1757. It is clear to see how the style of 50 years before has now become more formal and 'modern' looking, without changing much in essentials. This trooper of Frederick the Great's 10th Cuirassiers, the 'Gensd'armes', still wears a cocked hat lined with a steel cap, and a cuirass. The buff leather coat of the previous century, which was itself thick enough to turn some sword-cuts, has given way to a lavishly decorated coat, faced and laced in regimental colours: a typical feature of the 18th century's standing armies. This unit distinguished itself at the great victory of Rossbach where Gen. von Seydlitz led 33 cuirassier squadrons in a charge so devastating that when the battle was over the Prussians had lost only 548 men, and the French and Austrian enemy some 41,000, though the great majority were taken prisoner.

Left: Hussar of the Regiment de Rattsky in French service, c. 1720. This figure is taken from one of the earliest known paintings of Hungarian hussars recruited for service by the armies of the West. The unit was originally raised by the Elector of Bavaria, and passed to France in 1701. Many of the features of this peasant or 'cowboy' costume would become formalised in later generations. The fur-trimmed cap and short fur cape were in this period purely functional; and the colourful 'barrel-sash' may have begun life as spare reins and lariats wrapped round the waist for convenience.

Right: Hussar of the Hanoverian Regiment von Luckner, 1760. This German trooper shows off the splendidly flamboyant type of uniform typical of hussars in all armies of the late 18th and 19th centuries. The cap with fur trim has become a tall busby with a hanging 'bag'; the wolfskin, a slung *pelisse* over-jacket; the useful pouch on the sword-belt, a colourfully embroidered *sabretasche*; the strengthening-tape on the jacket front, a mass of rich decorative braiding.

how this happened. Very few people today have ever been in such a situation; but an idea of what it must have felt like can be gained by standing right up to the rails at a race meeting, so that the mass of jockeys and horses thunders past only a yard or two away. It is an experience to make anybody tremble, with an excitement which is at least half fear! Then try to imagine that the riders are not safely beyond the fence, but coming straight at you, eager to kill you. . . .

Blocks of steady, well-trained, confident infantry, who knew from long practice that they held weapons quite capable of killing or wounding the horses and riders before they could come within their own killing-range, might hold their ground despite their animal fright. For this reason, good cavalry generals did not charge steady, unbroken infantry: they charged infantry who were awkwardly placed, or confused by a change of direction, or in the middle of a manoeuvre, or already beginning to separate into disorganised clumps of men after being badly mauled by cannon or musket-fire. For the same reason, a good cavalry leader facing enemy horsemen never tried to hold off a charge with his own men sitting their horses

on the spot: he always tried to send them forward as fast as possible, to meet the charge on the move, so that the shock of meeting would be more or less 'equally divided'.

These facts were now clearly understood by all modern armies. Cavalry was still very important; but it had a part to play which was limited by the new weapons and new tactics. It could not charge the unbroken footsoldiers who made up the centre of the enemy army; but it could certainly mount flank attacks, unbalance the enemy line by driving away its own cavalry, and take any apportunity to exploit advantages won by infantry or artillery fire. It could not storm the sophisticated defences of 18th-century fortresses; but it was vital as the 'eyes and ears' of an army on the march, to scout out routes, probe enemy positions, and keep the enemy blinded by driving off his own mounted patrols. The aristocratic officers — who still clung to their old traditions, and who have always favoured service in the cavalry, in all armies — might not enjoy the freedom to ignore orders so typical of their armoured ancestors; but a free hand to raid behind an enemy army, cutting up their supply convoys and sowing terror and confusion, was still sheer heaven for a hot-blooded young nobleman with a regiment of light cavalry at his back! The cavalry might only rarely get the chance to make the decisive breakthrough in the centre of a battle; but there was nothing like cavalry for pursuing a beaten enemy, turning defeat into utter ruin by hounding retreating men until they scattered in terror and exhaustion.

Old duties, new names

This more professional and calculated view of the proper job of the cavalry produced, in the 18th century, the division of the mounted arm into different types of regiments. The main mass of heavy horse often kept the name — and the breastplates — of the old 'cuirassiers'. Two important new names were 'hussar' and 'dragoon'.

The true hussar was originally a wild-riding horseman on the plains of Hungary. Increasingly, European armies began to employ light units which aped the name, and a more organised form of the tactics, of these romantic raiders. They were the ultimate descendants of the ancient horse-archers of the East: 'the stinging flies', who avoided coming to grips, but who were very valuable as scouts, patrols, flank and rear-guards, hit-and-run raiders and merci-less pursuers. The hussars, in their wonderfully flamboyant uniforms, enjoyed the freedom to operate away from the main army; and unrivalled opportunities to swagger. They paid for these privileges with a short life expectancy. (A Napoleonic general remarked that any hussar who was not dead before his thirtieth birthday must be a blackguard!)

The 'dragoon' started life in the mid-17th century as an infantry musketeer mounted on a cheap, underbred horse purely for transport. Generals used his mobility to move him quickly wherever firepower was needed on the battlefield; he dismounted to fight on foot, with his horse held ready nearby. But during the 18th century dragoons came to be used more and more as conventional — though second-class — cavalry; and by the end of the century they were usually expected to be able to charge with the other regiments. At the same time they were still burdened with muskets, and were sometimes expected to fight as infantry. This confusion gave point to Dr. Johnson's sarcastic definition of a dragoon as 'a soldier that serves indifferently either on foot or on horseback'. By the height of the Napoleonic wars the name was all that separated the dragoons from other cavalry: they were simply all-purpose mounted troopers.

Left: Corporal, Royal Scots Dragoons, c. 1704.
Under Marlborough, the British army used dragoons as all-purpose troops, to some effect. At the storming of a fortress at Donauworth in 1704 Hay's Dragoons — later, the 'Royal Scots Greys' — rode forward into battle with *fascines* (bundles of brushwood) across their saddle-bows, and dropped them into a defensive ditch to make a bridge for the infantry. They then dismounted, and fought as infantry themselves; and when the enemy broke, mounted up and pursued them like cavalrymen! Note the slung musket, bayonet on the belt, and hatchet for 'pioneer' tasks, as well as the long sabre. Despite their wide usefulness, dragoons were still considered inferior to cavalry, and only earned 1s.6d. a day in contrast to the cavalryman's 2s.6d.

Right: French Dragoon, Régiment d'Autichamp, 1767.
A brass helmet with 'leopardskin' trim, green uniform, and musket would remain French dragoon distinctions (in developed forms) throughout the Napoleonic Wars.

Saddles and Bridles

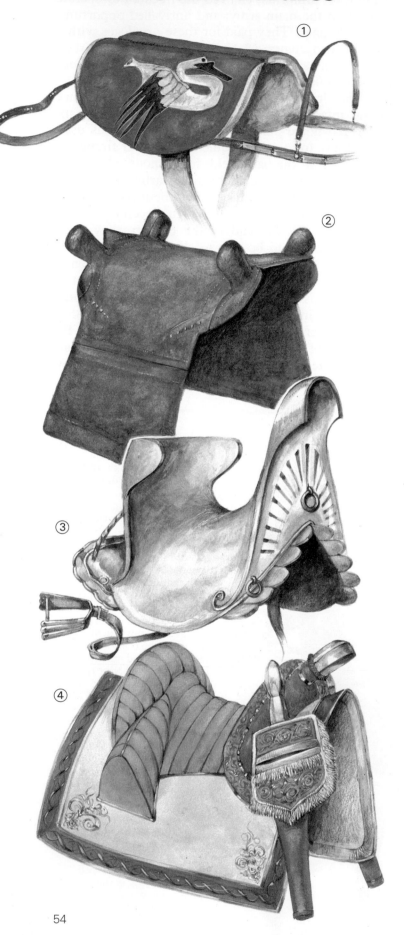

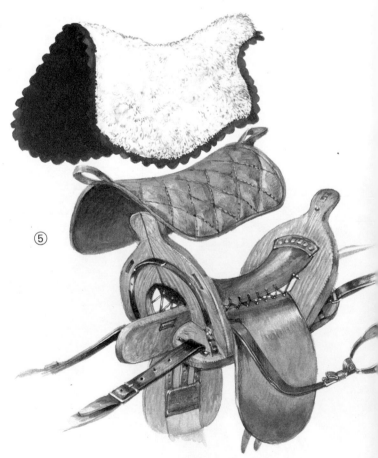

Any farm-bred child can demonstrate that just *riding* a tame horse does not require complicated 'horse furniture': a simple halter-rope to its head, and its own well-muscled back, are all the 'handle' and 'seat' a rider needs to jog comfortably over the fields. In ancient days most warriors actually fought bareback. Carvings show us that Hannibal's superb light cavalry from Numidia rode bareback, and controlled their horses without reins — the only 'saddlery and harness' they used was a rope round the beast's neck. Men like these did not need 'mechanical' controls over their horses: they made up for the lack of them by their intimate knowledge of, and daily contact with, the horses they raised and trained themselves.

For more heavily-equipped riders, who needed to stay on horseback for long periods, and whose lives might depend on the exact controlling of an excited horse in close combat, some kind of more stable seat, and some kind of reliable control over speed and steering were both necessary. The saddle and bridle evolved very early in the story of the horse soldier.

A pad strapped directly across a horse's back will cause painful sores on its spine. The Scythians of at least 500 years before Christ had already invented a saddle which solved this problem. Two cushioned pads, separate, but attached by straps or by wooden arches, will sit comfortably on the ridges of muscle each side of the horse's spine, supporting the rider and not injuring his mount. This is the basis of all saddles.

A more stable seat for a man who has to wield a weapon can be devised by raising the front and back of the saddle to give support, and by hanging stirrups from each side. A man braced between his feet in stirrups, and his lower back pressed into the high 'cantle' of a saddle, could keep his seat against the hardest blows.

Stirrups came on the scene surprisingly late. It is thought that they were invented — in wood and metal, anyway: simple rope loops would not survive to be found — in central Asia some time between the 1st and 4th centuries AD. Their arrival in the West was followed by the development of heavily armoured knights mounting 'shock' charges, but was probably not entirely responsible for the change. As we have seen, many ancient horsemen managed to charge without stirrups, gripping the horse tightly with their legs.

The 'bit' — a metal mouth-bar which enabled the rider to put unpleasant pressure on a horse's gums, and so to control his posture and speed — is a very old invention, dating from about 1400 BC. More complex types of bit, using the lever principle to pinch the horse's lower jaw between the mouth-piece and a chain passing below the chin, were certainly used by 300 BC. A combination of the simple 'snaffle' and the lever-action 'curb' was the standard military arrangement from the 18th century onwards.

Development of saddles and bridles over 2,000 years

1 Scythian saddle, 4th century BC, with two padded cushions.
2 Roman saddle cover, with four horns of leather stiffened with bronze, giving a stable seat. Like so much 'horse furniture', this was a Celtic invention.
3 Massive medieval saddle, almost enclosing the knight's pelvis to give great support against the shock of lance-charges and sword-fighting.
4 Comfortably-padded saddle of the 1600s, with slung pistols.
5 British Army saddle of 1814, 'exploded' to show the wooden 'tree', which sat on thickly folded blankets; the slung leather seat; and the sheep-skin cover, for comfort on the long rides a soldier faced on campaign.
6 'Snaffle' bit, dating back to about 1,400 BC. The pull of the reins presses it on the horse's gums, forcing the head up or down and controlling the horse's speed. Jointed types were harder for the horse to take between its teeth, to foil the rider's efforts at control!
7 'Curb' bit, invented by the Celts at least by 300 BC. The long cheek-piece acts as a lever round the fulcrum of the mouth-bar. Pulling the reins pinches gum and chin between the mouth-bar and the curb-chain passing under the chin. Some curbs were viciously cruel, being spiked and arched to hurt the gums and bruise the sensitive palate.
8 Most military bridles of the 18th-20th centuries had a combination of a 'snaffle' and a 'curb' and four reins. This gave very full control under all conditions. The type illustrated is the 1902 British Army model. The halter-rope was used for leading and tethering when the bridle and bits had been taken off, leaving only the simple headstall.

55

Soldat Lucien Defrère of the 7th Hussars, 1812

Every time the brown horse stumbled, Lucien feared that this time all his tugging and beating would not get it to its feet again. It was a miracle that the tormented creature had lasted this long: it had been living on snow-water and the bark off trees for days, and it had already been in a pitiful state when he found it. But to find it at all had been a sort of miracle in itself — and it made Lucien all the more determined that somehow, however many others died all around him, he was going to survive this nightmare retreat from Moscow.

Hardly any of the soldiers in the straggling ruins of Napoleon's Grand Army were still mounted. Back in June, when the Emperor had led his 450,000 men into Russia, he had some 80,000 cavalry. They were divided between the regiments of light horse attached to each infantry Corps; and the strong central reserve of cavalry which Napoleon had built up, during his dazzling career, as the decisive, mobile 'punch' which had set the seal on so many of his victories. Half of the reserve cavalry had been given to the dashing, outrageously vain Marshal Joachim Murat, a Gascon inn-keeper's son whose hot head and heart had raised him to the throne of Naples in his Emperor's service.

The reality of campaigning across the summer steppes had whittled that mighty force away with heart-breaking speed. The Russians fell back, trading

The classic French Napoleonic cavalry charge — the peak of the horse soldier's glory; one of the most exciting experiences of speed known to man before the invention of powered vehicles; and still, in the early 1800s, a battle-winning weapon.

Napoleon built up the small and unimpressive cavalry which he inherited into a very strong and well trained force. It was far more professional than the contemporary British cavalry, who were brave, well-mounted, but prey to Prince Rupert's old vice of never listening to the recall signal! While they charged off over the countryside (and, no doubt, while Cromwell turned in his grave!) the French would be kept well in hand, delivering repeated attacks where and when they were needed.

The core of Napoleon's horsed units were a dozen regiments of heavy cuirassiers. These, and other units of the central cavalry reserve which he always kept under his own hand, won him glittering victories at such battles as Marengo, Jena and Wagram. If launched at just the right moment, at an enemy line already shaken by infantry and artillery fire, a massed charge by many thousands of horsemen could break the enemy army in pieces: they nearly always ran before the terrifying wave of riders reached them.

But if trained, well-led foot soldiers had time to adopt an outward-facing square formation, then cavalry were almost useless against them. Simple arithmetic meant that at any time only about 20 riders had the space to charge one side of a square together, and thus faced between 100 and 200 muskets: suicide, for men and horses alike.

Squares *were* broken; but only if charged immediately after being raked by snipers or artillery, or if a freak accident — like a dying horse running blindly into their ranks — opened a gap for the troopers. It was still the *balanced* use of horse, foot and guns which won battles.

empty plains for time, and burning what they could not carry away. Feeding such a huge horse-herd, so far from their home depots, became a serious problem within weeks of the start of the advance. Foraging parties fanned out as far as 50 kilometres each side of the massive army, with scythes on their backs, searching for unfired grain to cut and sweet water to drink. As the army moved deeper into Russia, fighting inconclusive actions but never bringing the enemy to a pitched battle, the horses began to drop like flies. Kept saddled for 16 hours a day, overworked, and with only one veterinary surgeon for every 500 mounts, it was not surprising that they did.

The martyrdom of the horses

In the two months between the advance in late June and late August, Murat's command lost 18,000 out of 43,000 horses. They were so far from their depots that dismounted men, sent back towards Lithuania in a steady stream to pick up new mounts, never reappeared. Anything that could be caught locally was pressed into service — most of them underbred and undersized, so that huge cuirassiers rode stocky *panje* ponies with their stirrups almost touching the dust.

By the time old Kutusov stood and fought at Borodino in early September, barely half the cavalry were mounted. Lucien had fought on that dreadful field, in Jaquinot's Brigade out on the right wing. The 7th Hussars had been able to mount only two weak squadrons, a bare three months after crossing the border 1,100 strong. With the rest of the 1st Reserve Cavalry Corps they had charged the Russian Grenadiers south of the village of Semenovskaya, but without success. The steady Russian infantry squares had been impregnable — indeed, at one point the green-coated Grenadiers had even charged the impotent French cavalry at bayonet-point!

In late October, leaving empty Moscow burning, the Grand Army had tried to march south towards more realistic winter quarters; but now the Russians took the initiative, and harried them without mercy. The southward march was stopped dead at Vinkovo, where Murat's cavalry were horribly clawed, and fell back leaving 4,500 men dead or captured. Wearily, the remaining 90,000-odd Frenchmen, Germans, Italians, Portuguese, Belgians, Croats, Swiss, and other pressed levies of Napoleon turned on to the road of retreat westwards. The Cossacks gathered on their flanks like wolves: and on 5 November, the first snows fell. . . Within five days, another 30,000 horses died.

It was at Vinkovo that Lucien Defrère of the 7th Hussars' Elite Company had lost his own bone-weary mare to a Cossack lance. He would have died himself, spitted like a bug, if it had not been for Hans. And that was another reason why he was determined to keep this poor beast on its staggering legs for as long as possible, whatever cruelty it cost him. For Hans, tied now in its saddle, could no longer help himself.

Lucien had been lying stunned on the iron-hard dirt of Vinkovo, his legs tangled in poor old Honestine's spilled saddlery, while the fur-capped savage who had killed her rode round and round them, prodding with his lance, and laughing maliciously as he tried to get a clear thrust at the helpless Frenchman. He had been enjoying his game so much that he had not noticed, above the din of fighting, the one-man charge of the red-helmeted Hamburg trooper behind him, until Hans' lance had lifted him out of his own saddle as neatly as a pulled picket-pin. Hans, a grinning stranger in the soiled red and green finery of the 9th Light Horse Lancers, had reached down an arm to Lucien, shouting something that sounded vaguely encouraging in his outlandish foreign gabble. He had swept the shaken hussar up behind him, and ridden him to safety out of the mêlée. In the chaos of retreat, when it became clear that they had lost both the 7th Hussars and their brigade-mates of the Hamburg Red Lancers, Hans had still risked his own safety by carrying his new comrade double, for as long as his horse lasted.

Now, weeks later, somewhere on the featureless steppe between Orsha and the Beresina crossings, Hans was sick, starving, blind, and probably dying. They still had no more than a couple of dozen common words in any language. But Lucien had his pride; and if the German trooper was going to die, he would die moving westwards towards his distant home.

It was really Hans who had found this horse, in a way. They had both been afoot for more days than Lucien could remember, stumbling through the deepening snow and razor wind along a trail marked by corpses in fluttering rags. A few days past, Hans had gone snow-blind. They were both almost asleep as they walked, and Hans had wandered far off beside the ragged column before Lucien noticed, and went floundering after him. Not 20 metres beyond where his friend tripped and lay moaning in the fringe of a belt of trees, Lucien saw the brown horse standing with drooping head, its tail turned to the wind, and its reins locked in the frozen fist of the dead Chasseur officer who lay at its feet. Lucien had to break the leaden-grey fingers like twigs to free them; but he had seen too many horrors already to let that bother him. They had crossed the two-month-old battlefield of Borodino, for one thing: Lucien had been grateful for the snow that covered some of its worst sights.

In the past few days Lucien had seen men robbing fallen comrades, still living, of their last scraps of food — even of their coats and boots. He had seen them ignore the feeble appeals of mates who could go no further, and leave them by the side of the track for the lurking Cossacks. He had seen sick or wounded men, dragging themselves on hands and knees, crushed by riders and sledges who would not so much as swerve to avoid them. He had seen men who had lived with horses all their lives cut great collops of

meat from the haunches of living, staggering horses —
and seen the horses stumble on, apparently hardly
feeling the agony of their mutilation in the terrible
cold. He himself had stuck his knife into the brown
horse's flank and drained its warm blood into his
mess-tin, to cook into a sort of black pudding with a
handful of meal. The spectre of starvation does ugly
things to the most humane of men.

The supply system of Napoleon's armies was
basic in the extreme; and under conditions like those
encountered in Russia, it soon broke down completely. The bulk of the soldiers' rations were supposed to
come from 'living off the land'. In practice this meant
taking what they wanted from the countryside they
crossed, and leaving the wretched peasants to face
starvation themselves the coming winter. In 1812 the
Russian peasants had been forced by their rulers to
adopt the terrible but effective tactics of 'scorched
earth', practised since the days of Darius' war with the
ancient Scythians. The peasants still starved — but the
invader would starve with them.

The first troops to retreat through Smolensk had
almost emptied the storehouses left there during the
advance. For stragglers like Hans and Lucien there
had been hardly a handful left; the sack tied to their
saddle now contained perhaps a pound of grain-
sweepings from the corners of a granary floor, a few
strips of frozen horse-meat adhering to a badly scraped
hide, and a flask of brandy from the valise of the dead
Chasseur officer. But that same richly-dressed corpse
had provided Lucien with a fat purse of gold coins;
and as a careful soldier, Trooper Defrère had already
made plans for the future, when the brown horse
finally fell for the last time.

Equal shares in the horse's flesh, and 50 gold
francs — nearly six months' wages — were agreed as
the price for letting Hans join three ragged Saxons on
the one-horse sledge which lurched along nearby.
Lucien would have to walk beside it; but he had made
sure that the Germans knew his carbins was still in
good working order, and would be used at the first
sign of treachery. Lucien did not know how far they
still had to go before reaching the comparative safety
of Poland; but he was not going to let murder stop him
getting there, and taking Hans with him.

Even Lucien's iron determination might have
flagged had he known that there were still 60 miles to
go before they reached the Beresina bridges, where at
least 20,000 men would perish; or that another 200
miles lay between the Beresina and the last river
barring their escape from Russia — the Niemen. It
was perhaps fortunate that he did not know that of
450,000 men who had invaded Russia that spring, only
about 20,000 would survive. Of the 1,100-strong 7th
Hussars, just 20 mounted men, and 100 footsore
stragglers, would ever see the Polish border again.

In the Emperor's service

The cavalrymen who won military immortality in the armies of Napoleon were conscripts: men taken for army service by law, with no choice in the matter. Even so, their record proves that a combination of patriotism and training turned them into very fine soldiers indeed. Frenchmen of that period still saw themselves as sons of the Revolution — patriots, beset by foreign tyrants who were trying to strangle the first free Republic in Europe. The fact that Napoleon had turned that Republic into an Empire, ruled with all the cruel trappings of a military dictatorship, seems to have mattered little. Napoleon was one of the greatest geniuses in the history of warfare, and he led them to victory after victory. They paid a heavy price for their glory: of about 1,600,000 Frenchmen conscripted between 1800 and 1815, about a million died.

Men like Lucien Defrère — batchelors aged between 20 and 25 — had to report to their local authorities for a kind of lottery. One man in every seven was picked by lot; and from then onwards, until released by death, crippling wounds or the whim of his Emperor, he was destined to be a soldier. He was inoculated against smallpox; delivered to the barracks of his local regiment (in Lucien's case, the 7th Hussars' depot at Compiègne); entered on the rolls, and given a hot meal. The next day, confronted by a bewildering mountain of equipment for himself and his horse, and harried by shouting NCOs, he began to learn how to be a soldier.

The horses were paid for by the government. They were acquired by the individual regiments, either by direct purchase from merchants, or by 'requisition' — that is, they were seized in return for a paper promise that they *would* be paid for, at some time in the future. . . They were mostly three or four years old when bought in. The heavy Flemish and Norman breeds went to the cuirassiers; light cavalry made do with what was left, which often was not of high quality. The French always pressed into service the superior German horses they captured on the battlefield.

Lucien was paid one-third of a franc a day. Out of this he had to pay to repair or replace any item of equipment which he broke or lost. Some items, like belts and pouches, were supposed to last 20 years before needing replacement; and most parts of his uniform, between one and four years. It is not suprising that Lucien would soon have been heavily in debt to the government, and probably stayed that way throughout his service: a pair of shoes cost 18 days' pay, a pair of overalls 20 days', and even a tin of grease and a brush three days' pay! And Lucien needed a lot of grease — while cavalry service meant that he rode rather than marched across Europe, it also meant that he spent many hours each week in the barracks and stables cleaning and caring for the horse and its mass of harness. It has always been the cavalry's golden rule that the horse's health and comfort come before its rider's.

In barracks the cavalryman was entirely responsible for the care of his mount and the cleaning of its stable. Most troopers spent far more time with a dung-fork in their hands than a sabre or pistol! Though most recruits were still countrymen by birth — there were few large industrial cities — the army did not take their riding skills for granted. Riding-masters supervised long hours of training, often with the minimum of harness, until recruits were aching, saddle-galled and stiff in every joint! The results were worth the pain: in battle, in the exact formations and co-ordinated manoeuvres required of Napoleonic cavalry, a man's life — and his comrades' — depended upon disciplined horsemanship.

In the field, the care of the horse was supposed to come first, however tired the rider. In barracks the trooper's day was organised around the horse's feeding, watering, grooming and general comfort.

Napoleonic cavalry campaign equipment, similar for most armies:

British Light Dragoon, 1815

1 Slinging belt, with snap-hook, for .65-inch calibre Paget flintlock carbine; length 2 ft. 7 ins., weight 5 lbs. The ramrod is fixed to the muzzle by a swivel to prevent it being dropped and lost.

2 Wooden water canteen.

3 Linen haversack, for rations of bread and meat.

4 1796-pattern light cavalry sabre.

5 'Sabretasche': originally an all-purpose pouch, it was by now largely ornamental, and so slim it would hold only things like paper and writing equipment.

6 Forage net: on campaign, food for the horses was a constant problem, and grass would be cut wherever it could be found.

7 Tip of holster for flintlock New Land Service pistol, of same calibre as carbine.

8 Trooper's cloak, rolled and strapped to the saddle.

9 Sheepskin, with fancy edging in regimental colour. This was strapped over the saddle to give a more comfortable ride.

British Dragoon (2nd, or 'Royal Scots Greys'), 1815

10 1796-pattern heavy cavalry sword.

11 Ammunition pouch for pistol and carbine cartridges (30 rounds), which were both of .75-inch calibre in the heavy regiments; the pouch fits to a strap attached to the carbine slinging belt.

12 1796-pattern flintlock Dragoon carbine; length 3 ft. 6 ins., weight 8 lbs. The carbine could be unclipped from its sling and carried thrust under the cloak-roll strap, with its muzzle in a leather 'boot' hanging from the saddle.

13 Rolled-up forage net.

14 Rolled-up cloak.

15 One of two grain-sacks for the horse.

16 Spare horseshoe pouch.

17 Horse's nose-bag.

18 Valise — a cylindrical pack for the trooper's personal effects. This was in regimental colours, with a regimental device on the ends: here, 'RNBD' for the Royal Scots Greys' official title — 'Royal North British Dragoons'. Round the valise is rolled the painted canvas 'waterdeck', a rain-cover which protected the saddle when it was off the horse.

19 Trooper's mess-tin, in oilcloth cover.

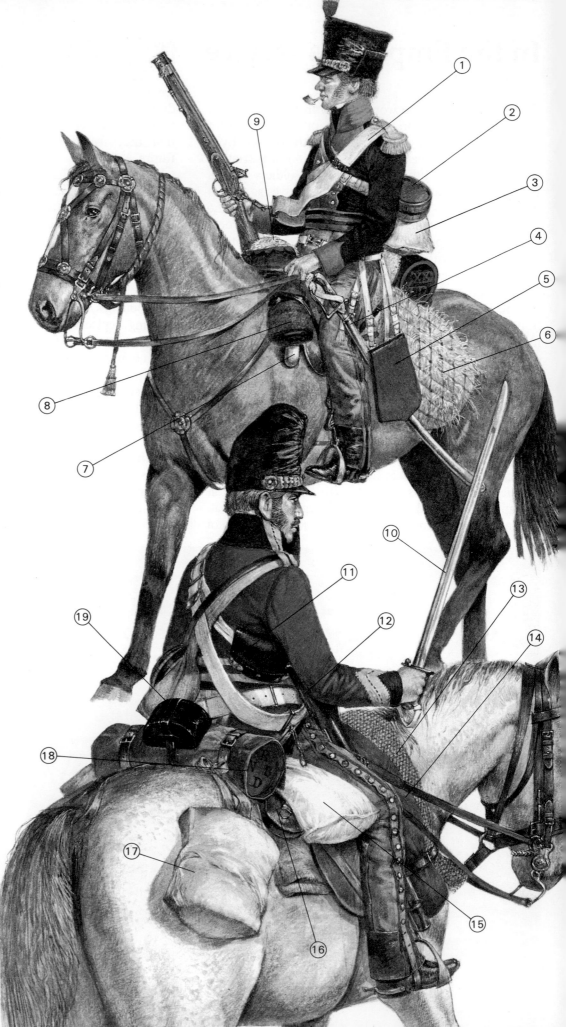

Peacocks of the Battlefield

The Napoleonic Wars saw the uniforms of European cavalry reach a peak of colourful flamboyance and variety. This 'butterfly collection' represents only a fraction of the dazzling range of military finery worn during this period.

1 *Russian Pavlograd Hussars.* The dish-topped *kiwer* shako was distinctively Russian. The front rank of a Russian hussar unit carried lances. In most armies the monarch's cypher was embroidered on the coloured saddle-cloth.

2 *Officer, Prussian 2nd or 'Death's Head' Hussars.* The sinister black uniform and skull-and-crossbones shako badge dated from the 1740s.

3 *Trumpeter, French 1st Hussars.* It was important for officers to be able to pick out trumpeters quickly, so that they could order urgent signals to be sounded; so in most armies their uniforms were particularly bright, often in colours reversed from those of the ordinary troopers.

4 *Officer, French Horse Grenadiers of the Imperial Guard.* This élite heavy cavalry unit wore deliberately austere uniforms, contrasting with the gaudy outfits of other troops.

5 *Standard-bearer, French Horse Chasseurs of the Imperial Guard.* The beautiful hussar-style uniform of an officer of this crack mounted bodyguard regiment, carrying the Eagle standard.

6 *Bavarian 1st Dragoons.* The tall leather helmet is distinctively Bavarian. Most cavalry of the day wore drab overalls, opening down the outside, to protect their breeches when on campaign.

7 *Officer, King's German Legion Dragoons.* The old-fashioned bicorn hat was still worn during the Peninsular War by British heavy cavalry, including this crack German volunteer unit.

8 *Polish Lancer of the French Imperial Guard.* The square-topped *czapka* helmet worn by this famous unit was later copied throughout Europe by lancers. Even today Polish troops wear a square-crowned field cap, descended from this headgear.

9 *Trumpeter, French 2nd Carabiniers.* From 1812 all French trumpeters were ordered to wear this green and yellow 'Imperial livery'.

Private George Broom of the 17th Lancers, 1854

George Broom and his horse Dasher died at almost the same instant, on 25 October 1854 in the North Valley before Balaclava in the Crimea. An egg-sized iron ball, one of a dozen from the last canister of case-shot fired by a terrified Russian gun crew in the battery drawn up across the eastern end of the valley, took Dasher in the front of the skull at about 100 yards range, braining him instantly. Since it struck at an acute angle it caromed off the bone even as it crushed it, and passed on through George's chest and out his back; he was dead before his body smashed into the ploughland like a limp doll, just in front of Dasher's huge, cartwheeling corpse. The Russians who had fired the shot had less than a minute left themselves before the lances and sabres of the maddened survivors of Captain White's squadron of the 17th Lancers stretched them reeking around the trail of their twelve-pounder.

The Russian gunners died because cavalry determined and disciplined enough could, in fact, charge head-on over two miles of open ground into the mouths of twelve heavy cannon, and reach the battery with enough men left in the saddle to slaughter the gunners. George died because the cost of such an insane charge was bound to be casualties of around 50 per cent of any unit which tried it. He died because the flustered, elderly commander-in-chief of the British army in the Crimea dictated a mudddled order; because his staff officer did not clarify it when writing it down; because the courier who carried it, and the divisional and brigade commanders who received it, were consumed by mutual dislike and personal quarrels; because the rigid code of behaviour among officers of an army which had changed little since Waterloo 40 years before held that to question an incompetent and suicidal order was cowardly.

George Broom was already an 'old soldier' when he died: of his 35 years, 18 had been spent in the army. He had been born in Bury Street, Stowmarket, a little country town in Suffolk in 1819. The years following the Napoleonic Wars were hard for country folk, and as a farm labourer George Broom's prospects were

grim. When the recruiting party came round East Anglia in the autumn of 1836, with their bugles, and fine beribboned uniforms, their free beer and freer promises, the 17-year-old George had not needed much persuasion. His enlistment bounty had been £5 15s. 6d. — but as the grinning sergeant with the huge whiskers had quickly explained, most of this was unfortunately held back to pay official expenses.

In his 18 years with the Lancers he had seen no real active service before he rode out from Preston Barracks in Brighton in April 1854 on the journey to Portsmouth and the troop ship for the Crimea. He had helped put down riots in the north of England and Ireland; but such scuffles hardly prepared him for the dreamlike horror of the last moments of his life.

Fiercely disciplined, and led today by a brave half-wit, the Brigade kept their pace controlled to a trot until the very last moments of their advance. They presented a slow, easy target for the cannon and massed infantry muskets which tore into them from three sides. By the time he kicked into a full gallop George was beyond a simple emotion like fear: he was shocked, deafened, and almost out of touch with reality. His only conscious sensation was the deep hunger to get close enough to the enemy to kill them. The ghastly deaths and mutilations he had seen all round him, in brief flashes, as he rode down the valley

had ceased to seem real at the moment when he glanced aside and saw Sergeant Talbot keeping pace with him: lance firmly braced, rigid in the saddle — and headless. . . . With a shout of triumph George Broom galloped into the smoke, and the canister-shot, accompanied by a riderless horse and a headless sergeant. Beyond the smoke he passed at once into history; and, perhaps unfortunately, into legend.

Of 673 officers and men of the Light Brigade who had paraded that morning, 303 were killed, maimed, or captured during the brief attack; 460 of their horses were killed or badly hurt. Of the 146 officers and men of the 17th Lancers who followed Captain Morris in the charge, some 75 men, and less than 50 horses, survived in one piece.

The only good which might have come out of this slaughter would have been for it to become instantly and universally infamous as a proof of incompetence and the futile waste of lives. Instead, it was quickly wrapped up in the 'cavalry mystique', and served up to the onlooker as an example of self-sacrificing courage. Behind the sonorous verses of 19th century military legend, we can still hear an old enemy: the murderous vanity of Jean de Boisvert and his fellow barons, who would rather die, defeated but splendid, than win at the cost of applying such a middle-class quality as intelligence!

Corporal Willi Vogler of the United States 3rd Cavalry, 1876

'*F*orm skirmish line! Horse-holders to de rear!'
Thinking, as usual, in his native German, Willi has a moment to reflect that after so many crippling months in the saddle trying to find the elusive Cheyenne bucks and bring them to battle, he really ought to be happy to see them at last. Unfortunately, his first glimpse is of a fast, loose skein of about twenty painted riders bent over the necks of their ponies, and coming whooping straight for the creek-bank where he and his dozen troopers have dismounted for a brew of coffee. The prairie out here north of the Rosebud River was as empty as a billiard table five minutes ago. Now, as he kneels to squint along the barrel of his carbine, and tries to steady his breathing long enough to take aim, Willi has more immediate problems than wondering if Captain Mills will be pleased with his report of contact.

At least the army in which he enlisted four years ago, as a penniless immigrant from Hesse, has learned something about how to fight these quick-silver tribesmen. Even back in the Civil War the US Cavalry grasped that charges with sabre and pistol might look wonderful in an oil-painting, but were no way to fight an enemy who refused to play by the same rules. As his little line of Irish, German, Swedish and American-born troopers kneels nervously in the grass, every fourth man drags four of their mounts back down the creek-bank, where they will be safer from the bullets

and arrows, but handy for flight or pursuit if needed in a hurry. Willi fervently hopes it will be pursuit. The Springfield carbine is a single-shot weapon; but its 'trap-door' breech takes a heavy, .45-calibre brass cartridge, and at this range even his troopers — limited to 90 rounds a year for practice — ought to be able to make their shots count.

Soldiering on the Plains

Willi's troopers are a hard-bitten, cynical bunch. They enlisted for five years, on pay of thirteen dollars a month — when it ever arrives. They had virtually no training before being sent to join their understrength units, scattered in isolated one-Troop forts along immense frontier of America's westward expansion into Indian territory. They spend most of their service labouring, or riding fruitless patrols over hundreds of miles of wilderness. Their ramshackle forts are sweltering in summer, freezing in winter. Their officers tend to be grey-haired Civil War veterans far too old for their ranks, who have given up hope of promotion in this small, miserly army — and who are not the kindest of commanders, in consequence. The food is salt pork, beans, rice, hard-tack biscuit, and 'coffee that would grow whiskers on a cannon-ball'. There is nothing to spend the miserable pay on but rot-gut whisky, which is probably safer to drink than the water. Little wonder that nearly half of the army

are foreign-born, or illiterate drifters: only the desperate would enlist for this life. Even so, many of them soon change their minds. Last year the 3rd Cavalry lost about 150 deserters — out of a total strength of 650.

It is only when they are gathered for large mobile columns on summer campaign — like this one, commanded by General Crook — that the dispersed units of each twelve-Troop regiment even serve together. Two or three columns of cavalry, infantry and light artillery criss-cross the prairie on converging courses, trying to trap the Indian bands into pitched battles, but seldom succeeding. The Indians travel light, and can live off the land which they know so well. The immigrants and town-born Americans of the cavalry travel much slower; each horse carries 100 lbs of rations and equipment, and even so the troopers cannot venture far from the lumbering supply waggons.

If the Indians ever do find themselves hard pressed, they simply scatter into small, elusive groups. If the soldiers disperse in their turn, to follow up each faint trail, then they are liable to get ambushed — like Corporal Vogel's squad. Man for man, the Indian brave is a better horseman, a better fighter, and far better at using the land and the elements to his advantage. Willi's army has on its side the dogged, disciplined approach of the white man's society; it will

stick to its task, however many times it fails, until the Indian is tamed or wiped out. The brave, spirited, undisciplined individuals of the Indian tribes cannot match this steamroller determination; and in the end, it will grind them down. They cannot understand the concept of taking, and owning forever, areas of the earth – the earth that the Great Spirit gave to all creatures, to wander over and use according to their needs. This war-party do not look beyond the hope of beating this particular group of white men.

In this lonely fight, north of the Rosebud, Willi's dust-caked troopers have the advantage of better guns, more ammunition — and such discipline in acting together, on command, as a keen captain and a gruff Hessian corporal have managed to knock into them.

The accuracy of the next dozen shots they fire will decide whether they have something to boast about when they rejoin their Troop tonight; or whether they are going to die, horribly, out here on the empty plains. But whether they live or die, they are going to be important in the history of the horse soldier. Although George Broom was still alive when they were children, they are soldiers of another age. They are, in fact, 'mounted infantry'; and only horsemen who can find their enemy, and then swing down from the saddle to fight on their knees with rifles, have any serious future in the world's armies.

The Imperial Auxiliaries, 1850–1914

During the second half of the 19th century, while the United States was fighting on its own internal frontier, the European powers who were conquering colonial empires in Asia and Africa were also coming to grips with new kinds of warfare. The traditional stately dance of horse, foot and guns might still be thought suitable for campaigns against 'civilised' enemies like the Russians in the Crimea. But against the hit-and-run tactics of tribal enemies lurking in the desert, the jungle, or the wild mountain passes of the imperial frontiers, such methods and means were not often possible.

Imperial campaigns tended to be fought by small forces, by European standards. There were few roads to move on, and few sources of everyday needs: everything had to be carried with the army, in waggons which were limited to the few possible routes. The advantages of increasingly modern firearms, and disciplined marksmanship, usually outweighed the wild courage of the tribesmen in pitched battles; but most campaigning was — as in America — a matter of patrolling, and of swift punitive columns. All the imperial powers realised the usefulness in this sort of fighting of locally-recruited horsemen.

Native regiments of cavalry, serving under a mixture of their own tribal leaders and white officers, were soon found in the colonial armies of Britain, France, Spain and Italy. They were inexpensive; they did not need much equipment issued, beyond guns and ammunition; their death in action or from disease did not cause trouble among the voters at home in Europe;

Top: Corporal, French 3rd Chasseurs d'Afrique; Algeria, 1855. When they first invaded Algeria in the 1830s the French began by raising units of Europeans — Zouave infantry, and Chasseurs d'Afrique cavalry — specially for colonial service. Recruitment of local warriors — Tirailleur infantry, and Spahi cavalry — soon followed.

Left: British officer, 10th Lancers (Hodson's Horse); India, 1912. One of many regiments of Indian cavalry, this was originally raised at the time of the 1857 Mutiny from among loyal Sikhs. It saw action both on the North-West Frontier and in Africa. British officers started to adopt native parade uniforms in about 1900.

and above all, they brought to the fight against the tribes an expert knowledge of local tactics, and of the ground. In fact, they were the exact descendants of Rome's Thracian mercenary cavalrymen like Titus Flavius Bassus.

The European armies sent strong forces of their own 'line' regiments out to their colonies to provide the heavy, ponderous, massively armed core of the frontier garrisons; but since most warfare was mobile and on a small scale, the native regiments saw a great deal of action. They therefore attracted ambitious and adventurous European officers; and, in time, from being slightly despised auxiliaries, they became 'fashionable'. The romantic image of these partly tamed and often extremely loyal native cavalrymen became popular in Europe. Jingling squadrons, dressed in superbly exotic uniforms based on what had originally been everyday native dress, began to attract attention in European parades and jubilees.

In the field, these light horse regiments were usually very effective. Combining European discipline and organisation with the fire and cunning of centuries of local tribal warfare, they began to teach the European troops, by example, how best to fight in wild country against elusive guerilla enemies. By the turn of the 19th century they were mostly used as 'mounted infantry'. It was on the imperial frontiers that far-sighted officers of the European armies learned the skills that the Americans learned in the Indian Wars: the use of the horse merely as transport to get to the chosen battlefield quickly, before the enemy could fade away; the use of baggage-mules instead of ponderous waggons; the use of ground, light and weather in a deadly game of hide-and-seek; and the importance, even for 'cavalrymen', of good individual marksmanship, since most actions were fought out by snipers among the rocks and trees.

Top: Italian Savari; Libya, 1930s. These irregular desert horsemen raised in Italy's North African colonies wore entirely native dress, and provided their own mounts and equipment. Only the uniform black *burnoose* robe, and the Italian carbine, were issued to them by the Army.

Right: French lieutenant, 6th Algerian Spahis; Morocco, 1930s. Arab troopers and NCOs wore native-style uniforms; French officers wore this romantic mixture of European and Arab styles. His insistence on wearing this tunic in action earned a famous French officer, Capt. de Bournazel, the nickname of 'The Red Man'. It also got him killed, in Morocco in 1933.

The Last Muster,
1914–1918

Men of the British 17th Lancers on the Western Front, 1917–18. In the 50 years before Pte. George Broom of the 17th rode to his death at Balaclava, resplendent in blue and gold and carrying a lance, the appearance and tactics of his regiment had changed hardly at all. Just 60 years after his death they had become drab, masked, and largely irrelevant ghosts.

Nobody will ever know how many horses died in the First World War: the number must be in millions. The British Army in Europe alone lost 256,000 dead, and more than two and a half million horses and mules passed through the military veterinary hospitals. The slaughter among soldiers was so appalling that the survivors determined that never again should a war be fought in this way. The slaughter among the animals proved to all but the most unimaginative and stony-hearted that the cavalry horse no longer had any business in the front lines. (But it should not be forgotten that this was not the first time that the British horse soldier's mount had paid a ghastly price; in the Boer War in South Africa at the turn of the century at least 350,000 cavalry horses died.)

When the great powers allowed themselves to drift into war in 1914, it was believed that this would be simply an old-fashioned campaign of manoeuvre on a huge scale. But within weeks it became clear that something had changed: something which cancelled out the lifelong experience of the generals, and which they were never able to come to terms with.

The advances which had been made in the technology of killing in the years since the last European war had upset forever the balance between horse, foot and guns which had more or less held good since the days of Gustavus Adolphus 300 years before. The foot and the artillery now had weapons of such terrible power — accurate high-explosive shells of long range, and reliable rapid-fire machine guns — that the cavalry simply could not live on the same battlefield.

These weapons, and above all the machine gun, had put the advantage in battle firmly into the hands of the defender rather than the attacker. They turned the open ground between opposing armies into a fire-swept killing ground which no attacker could cross without suffering monstrous losses. Before the first winter of the war the fighting was deadlocked. The armies faced one another from deep trenches across a narrow strip of shell-churned no-man's-land; only by huddling below ground could the infantry survive the storm of artillery fire and the lash of the machine guns.

The unbreakable barrier

The generals saw this stalemate as temporary. Their training taught them that the only way to win was to outflank or breach this solid belt of defences, so that cavalry could pour through into the enemy's rear and panic him into retreat. But the trenches stretched unbroken from the Dutch coast to the Swiss border, in a broad scar right across Europe; they could not be outflanked. So the infantry were condemned to a series of massed frontal assaults in a vain attempt to blast a gap in the front. For four nightmare years they tried, both supported and martyred by huge artillery bombardments. Tens of thousands of men died in the evil swamp of shell-holes or hanging on the cruel barbed wire entanglements, and all for a few hundred yards of ground — which were usually recaptured, within days, at a cost of yet more tens of thousands of lives. The gap was never made; and meanwhile the cavalry waited, often under the same rain of shells which slaughtered the infantry. In 1916 there were reckoned to be a million cavalry horses in the front lines. Their presence was simply irrelevant — but that did not stop them dying.

It was not so much the unbroken barrier of wire and trenches which made the cavalryman helpless; it was the machine-gun. In the first weeks of war, while movement was still possible, there was proof of this on those occasions when cavalry following the traditional tactics came in contact with infantry armed with machine-guns, and supported by modern field artillery. The results for the cavalry were too horrible to be described.

On those few occasions when local successes by infantry — in the later years, supported by the first generation of tanks — did blast a narrow corridor through the trenches, it was found that the cavalry still could not 'exploit forward' with the mobility which was supposed to be their strength. Horsemen were actually *slower* than footsoldiers when faced by any degree of opposition. An infantryman under machine-gun fire could take cover in a shell-hole until the enemy had been silenced: a horse could not. The effective range of modern weapons was so great that these huge, helpless, terrified targets had to be pulled right out of the battle if they were to survive at all.

The generals, raised in the old tradition, were obsessed with keeping the cavalry intact for the breakthrough which never came. They could not grasp that this ignoble grovelling in holes in the ground was the pattern of future warfare: insisting that it was a temporary pause in the 'proper' conduct of war, they clung to their belief in the 'moral superiority' of a brave man with a sword in his hand, riding a well-bred horse in a knee-to-knee charge with hundreds like him. That a soulless metal machine like a Maxim gun could cancel out a thousand years of military tradition overnight was more than they could bear to face. Their wilful blindness would be almost comic, if it had not cost such a hideous price in dead men and horses.

The inactivity of most cavalry units did not save their horses. Three-quarters of the dead mounts died from disease and exposure, for there were few stables in the war zone. Picketed in the rain and cold, with no shelter but a sodden blanket, the horses died like flies from the wide range of illnesses to which all horses are easy prey.

Apart from the cavalry, the artillery and supply units used hundreds of thousands of draft horses to pull their guns and waggons. These poor beasts died horribly under shell-fire or poison gas attack, leaving every road in the battle zone lined with a pathetic jumble of corpses.

The final victory

The generals' refusal to accept that the day of the cavalryman was over was stiffened by one campaign where cavalry were successful — though for purely local reasons. In the Middle East General Allenby's army contained a strong force of British, Indian and Australian cavalry. Fighting in open country against the weakened Turkish Army, with open flanks to be turned and few strong, fixed defence lines to face, these hardy troopers played an important part in the victories of 1918. Although the Australians had shown their strength as 'mounted infantry' horsemen in South Africa in 1900–01, they now found themselves riding in the occasional old-fashioned cavalry charge.

The achievements of this last true cavalry army had no lessons to teach about the future of warfare in Europe, however. The 'horse soldier' must say farewell, at last, to his horse, and face war's horror alone — inside a mechanical steel box. Like the knight of old, he must rely upon armour to protect him if he was to move with the freedom needed for the traditional cavalry tasks.

Left: Lieutenant-colonel of French cuirassiers, 1914; and lieutenant of 'foot cuirassiers', 1915. The essentially Napoleonic uniform, with helmet and cuirass covered to stop them flashing, soon gave way to the universal 'horizon blue'. Many dismounted units were only distinguishable by their odd helmet — the old type, but with the crest removed, and the surface camouflaged with blue paint or a cloth cover.

Below: At Beersheba, Palestine on 31 October 1917 the 4th and 12th Australian Light Horse of Allenby's Desert Mounted Corps took the town and its 700-strong Turkish garrison by an old-style cavalry charge. Lacking sabres, they used their rifles and fixed bayonets instead. The Turks had few machine guns, so the Aussies were able to reach and jump the first trench, penetrating quickly into the enemy position.

Exchanging 'Violins' for 'Gramophones', 1920–1940

A Rolls-Royce armoured car passes British cavalry on the North-West Frontier of India in the late 1920s.

Despite the painfully obvious lesson of the First World War — that horsed cavalry had no place on the modern battlefield — the change from horses to armoured vehicles between the World Wars was slow and grudging. It was accepted partly because the job of light armoured vehicles was reconnaissance and raiding, the traditional cavalry task; and partly because if the cavalry had not accepted it, they knew they might be disbanded altogether, and simply turned into infantry.

As late as 1926 Field Marshal Haig, who as British commander-in-chief on the Western Front had presided over the death of a generation in the machine-gun-swept desolation between the trenches, was to write that 'aeroplanes and tanks are only accessories to the man and the horse . . . as time goes on you will find just as much use for the well-bred horse as you have ever done. . .'

It is easy to mock this sort of hopeless blindness. It is kinder to remember that to a generation of soldiers who had grown up to love horses and honour the age-old traditions, the idea of discarding them for noisy, dirty, dead machines was as painful (in the words of one observer) as asking a great musician to throw away his violin and devote himself in future to a gramophone.

The change was delayed by the fact that under certain special, local circumstances horses were still useful. On the frontiers of the colonial empires, where roads were few and tribesmen without modern weapons fought hit-and-run campaigns, cavalry used as fast-moving 'mounted infantry' were as effective as they had been for half a century; though even here, armoured cars and aircraft soon showed that they could do the same job more economically. In some backward countries, such as Russia during the civil wars of the 1920s, large cavalry forces still had a part to play — but only because these were basically 19th century wars of sweeping movement over huge areas, with few fixed defence lines guarded by

wire, artillery and machine guns.

The same was true of the isolated cases where cavalry saw action during the early years of the Second World War. In Poland in 1939, despite the legends to the contrary, the lancers did not charge German tanks; they dismounted and fought as infantry. British horsed cavalry saw limited use in Syria and Persia in 1940–41; and even the mighty Wehrmacht still fielded a few cavalry divisions during their advance into Russia in 1941–42, though they were soon relegated to anti-partisan patrols behind the front lines.

Of the major nations, only Soviet Russia still had large cavalry forces — scores of thousands of riders, who were surprisingly successful at disrupting their more up-to-date enemy by making surprise raids on German rear areas. These descendants of the Mongol hordes, travelling great distances on their hardy ponies, could hook between the widely dispersed German columns under cover of night, or in weather that brought motor vehicles to a halt. They often managed to spread panic

out of all proportion to their strength: there was apparently something so ancient and horrible about the prospect of being cut down in an ambush by a sabre-swinging Cossack that it made the Germans' flesh creep. Even so, cavalry who confronted modern troops in any but these special circumstances were still doomed to disaster.

There is still a raging argument about the identity of the cavalry unit which made the last traditional, knee-to-knee charge in battle. A tiny group of Indian troopers of the Burma Frontier Force charged when they fell into a Japanese ambush at Toungoo, Burma, on 21 March 1942; but the honour apparently goes to the Italian 'Savoia' Dragoons. Serving in Russia alongside their German allies, the regiment sent part of their strength into a mounted attack with sabres and hand grenades at the village of Ischbuschenskij on 24 July 1942. The charge, co-ordinated with a dismounted attack by the rest of the unit, was apparently successful; though very costly.

The last generation of horsed cavalrymen:

1 *French Foreign Legion cavalryman in Syria, 1927.* Most European armies still found a use for cavalry in the desolate, trackless terrain of their imperial colonies during the 1920s and 1930s. Even here, however, most of the actual fighting was done with rifle, maching-gun and grenade by dismounted troopers; the horses were simply their means of transport, and were kept safely to the rear once battle was joined.

2 *Officer of Spanish Moroccan Cavalry, mid-1930s,* in the splendid parade uniform so typical of European colonial troops since the 19th century. Cavalry was used to some extent during the Spanish Civil War of 1936–39.

3 *Cossack in German Service, 1943.* The hundreds of thousands of Soviet troops who voluntarily changed sides during the German invasion included enough Cossacks to form two cavalry divisions. These minority peoples from the southern USSR saw the Soviets as cruel foreign occupiers.

4 *Polish Lancer, 1939.* Poland's 40 cavalry regiments fought bravely against German invasion, but almost entirely on foot. Tales of lancers charging Panzer tanks are untrue: the Poles were courageous, but not insane.

5 *Standard-bearer, Italian 3rd 'Savoia' Dragoons, 1942.* Serving in Russia in July 1942, a squadron of this regiment may have made the last true sabre-charge by a formed cavalry unit.

Steel Stallions, 1939–45

While these few odd corners of the Second World War sheltered the last surviving war horses, the vast majority of 'cavalrymen' fought their campaigns inside the mobile, armoured gun-carriages which they had so reluctantly entered in the 1930s. Pinning their ancient badges defiantly to the oily black cap of the tank crewman, the 'troopers', 'riding-masters', 'cornets', 'lodging-marshals' and 'corporals of horse' clung to every outward tradition they could. The regiments often kept their old names — cuirassiers, lancers, dragoons and hussars are with us to this day, though they ride 40-ton steel monsters breathing deisel-fumes. The cavalry still tended to attract the more languid young officer from the landed gentry, with his easy air of inherited authority, and his studied refusal to appear to take his profession seriously. But the yellow bandanas, the clanking and thundering 'sabre squadrons' of 40-ton 'chargers', and all the other affectations were harmless enough; the world had rolled on, and the dead hand of cavalry stubborness could do little damage now.

As far as the old tasks of the horse soldier still existed, the newly armoured regiments performed them. The reconnaissance patrol was carried out in light, manoeuvrable armoured cars and half-tracks, which had little protection against serious opposition, but which could carry the 'hussars' and 'chasseurs' out of trouble as rapidly as they had got into it. Where a massed charge by 'shock cavalry' might break an enemy's front on the more fluid and less deeply dug-in lines favoured during this war, then the heavy tank wedge took the part of the ranks of 'cuirassiers'. Mounted infantry 'dragoons' rode in trucks, or tracked armoured personnel carriers. It was now the armour which ranged through the enemy's rear areas to panic him into rout, and which lurked concealed on the tail of a retreat to discourage too close pursuit. In the fast, free-ranging, self-contained armoured columns of the German *blitzkrieg*, slashing into enemy country at widely separated points, we see the perfection of the Mongol *tuman* of pony-riders.

Echoes of old companionship

Though four or five men now shared a mount of dead steel rather than living horseflesh, the descendants of the horse soldiers still sentimentalised over their chargers. A crew would often give their tank a name; they would grow to recognise the individual vices and strengths of their particular machine, and curse or praise them as if they were the wilful habits of a living beast. The comparison was not so far-fetched. The troopers of the old days were countrymen, who had grown up familiar with horses and their ways; the tank crews were often conscripts from the streets of industrial towns, who were as familiar with the quirks of motor vehicles. The fact that the tank provided not just a fighting platform, but also a moving home on campaign, increased its crew's fondness for this mass-produced metal machine.

Like the horseman, the tank crew paid for the advantage of not having to walk to war. Like the horse, the tank was a big and obvious target, and hiding it on the battlefield was seldom possible. It might give power and speed, but it also drew the enemy's fire more than the scurrying footsoldier. A shot and falling horse might crush its rider's leg, or throw him to the ground with bone-breaking force. A 'brewed up' tank would often burn with terrifying speed, its small and awkward hatches trapping the crew to roast alive in the flames of ammunition and fuel. It can have been little consolation to reflect that the tank, unlike the horse, did not share its master's agony when their luck ran out.

'Horse soldiers' today

The biggest change in the nature of the 'horse soldier' since the Second World War is probably his standard of education. In the tank crewman of today are found the skills once expected only of the engineer and the artillery officer, as well as those of the field-crafty fighting man. The incredible increase in the complexity of his 'mount' makes this inevitable, and is reflected in its cost. Three hundred and forty years ago a trooper who rode with 'Corporal Whitton' went to war on a horse costing the equivalent of about ten weeks' pay for a common soldier. In the 1980s a heavy tank costs about the same as a soldier's pay for 30 years!

While the 'cavalry' of most modern armies now man tanks of space-age complexity and cost, some other units have been 'converted' into airborne troops. Riding to wherever they are needed in helicopters, they dismount to fight like the dragoons of old. Their flying mounts give them tremendous mobility; but their job remains more or less what it always was for light cavalry — to turn up unexpectedly, and hit the enemy from an inconvenient direction.

If these parallels between the genuine cavalry of old and the mechanical armies of today seem to be unrealistically strained, then the soldiers themselves must bear the responsibility for reminding us of their ancestry. On the uniform of the American helicopter-riders of the 1st Cavalry Division (Air Mobile) is still to be seen a patch shaped like a knightly shield, in the traditional cavalry yellow, and bearing a black horse's head. On the turret of Britain's massive new Challenger tank may be seen an insignia carefully added by the Royal Hussars: their badge of the 'Prince of Wales's feathers', which can be traced back to the shield blazon of the blind King John of Bohemia who rode to his death at Crécy in 1346.

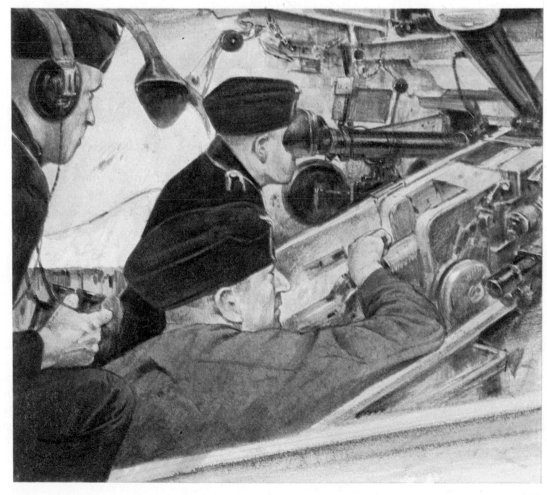

Left: US Army Sherman tank crew doing the maintenance work which kept them from their few hours' sleep each night. Like the trooper of old, the 'tanker' had to feed, water, rub down, and 'clean the hooves' of his mount before eating or resting himself. To refuel a Sherman took 35 heavy 5-gallon cans. Tanks carried some 90 shells, each weighing about 20 lbs, which had to be manhandled through small hatches. The complex wheel and track mechanism needed daily attention and greasing.

Right: Panzer III tank crew of the German 24th Armoured Division, converted from cavalry only in 1941. Tank crews lived, travelled, fought, and often ate and slept in a cramped steel box full of sharp edges. They froze in winter and baked in summer. The din of the engine and gun deafened them. Violent motion, in a vehicle without windows, caused nausea; and the gun filled the tank with dizzying fumes. If an enemy shell penetrated the armour, the stored shells often blew up too fast for the crew to escape.

Throwbacks and Legends

Even in this age of nuclear missiles and 'Star Wars' machinery, the horse can still occasionally be found carrying men into battle. In guerilla campaigns in desert or thickly-wooded country they still have advantages for 'mounted infantrymen'. Tracked vehicles are large, noisy, and impossible to hide. A horseman can sometimes slip along narrow bush trails unseen and unheard; he has much greater speed and mobility than a foot soldier, a better view from high in his saddle, and is not tired out by marching over broken ground for hours before he gets near the enemy. While these 'counter-insurgency' horsemen usually dismount to fight in classic 'mounted infantry' fashion, the surprise encounters inevitable in this kind of war have led to isolated cases where soldiers have charged into action firing modern automatic weapons from the saddle.

Right: Major, Grey's Scouts; Rhodesia, 1978

Below: Quartermaster, Mounted Platoon, French Naval Infantry Half-Brigade; Algeria, 1958

There is no doubt that warriors have cherished a special love for their horses down the centuries. It goes beyond the simple affection felt for a pet. Men have spoken of the warhorse like a human comrade, as if it *chose* to go into battle in their cause. When this silly, but natural illusion gets mixed up with admiration for the horse's beauty and strength, its grace and spirit, the result can be wonderful poetry:

Hast thou given the horse strength? Hast thou clothed his neck with thunder?. . . The glory of his nostrils is terrible. He paweth in the valley, and rejoiceth in his strength: he goeth on to meet the armed men. He mocketh at fear, and is not afrighted; neither turneth he back from the sword. . . He swalloweth the ground with fierceness and rage. . . He saith among the trumpets, Ha, ha; and he smelleth the battle afar off, the thunder of the captains and the shouting. (Job 39: 19–25)

Legendary war-leaders have always been regarded with a sort of half-magical reverence; and this feeling is sometimes extended to include the leader's horse, the partner in his greatest exploits. In ancient times much was written about Bucephalus — 'Oxhead' — the Thessalian stallion which Alexander the Great rode in most of his victories. Already 14 years old, and an unmanageable brute, when the 12-year-old Macedonian prince astonished his father

by taming him, Bucephalus lived to a great age. He was cossetted and spoilt, and ridden only in battle; and he is supposed to have been about 30 when he finally died after the battle of the Hydaspes in India. Once, when he was captured in an ambush by Caucasus Mountain tribesmen, Alexander threatened wholesale massacre if he was not returned — which he quickly was! When he died, the conqueror founded a whole city around his tomb.

Another legendary steed was Babieca, who carried Spain's national hero Rodrigo de Bivar — 'El Cid' — in his 11th-century wars against the Moors. When Rodrigo finally died inside besieged Valencia, he left orders for his embalmed and armoured corpse to be tied in Babieca's saddle; and the dead hero led a last victorious cavalry charge astride his faithful steed.

Even in more modern and less superstitious times, the horses of famous generals have attracted great interest. Napoleon's Marengo, Lee's Traveller, Grant's Cincinnati, Stonewall Jackson's Little Sorrel — all these horses became the subjects of stories and gossip. When the Duke of Wellington's Copenhagen finally died, after comfortable years as a family pet, this 'veteran of Waterloo' was buried with military honours and given an obituary in *The Times*!

A sort of cult of 'animal heroism' has also gathered around horses which have survived terrible wounds. When, in 1982, an IRA murder gang planted bombs in London which killed several Army bandsmen and Household Cavalry mounted guardsmen and their horses, and maimed others horribly, the greatest public interest centred not around dead or mutilated soldiers, but around the recovery of a horse named Sefton. One of the most famous examples of this irrational but powerful sentiment makes a pleasant story with which to end a book in which we have had to mention all too many horses cruelly slaughtered.

When the relief force arrived on the dreadful field of Custer's Massacre near the Little Bighorn River in June 1876, the only living member of the US 7th Cavalry which they found among the dead was Comanche, the 14-year-old 'buckskin' horse of Captain Keogh, commander of 'I' Troop. Although he had 12 arrow and bullet wounds, and would normally have been shot, it became a matter of pride to the 7th Cavalry's farrier to save this last survivor of the battle. He was taken back to Fort Abraham Lincoln with great care, and lovingly tended for a year before he could leave the veterinary hospital.

Comanche lived as the regiment's cherished mascot until 1891. He lived in a special stall; was spoilt and petted by all ranks; was never ridden, and did no work. He only paraded on ceremonial occasions, when he was led saddled, bridled, but riderless with 'I' Troop. He had the run of the fort — and was the scourge of the officers' flower gardens!

Glossary

Alexander the Great, 356–323 BC: King of Macedonia, and conqueror – in just 12 years – of the whole eastern Mediterranean world, the Persian Empire, and Asia as far east as north-west India.

Asclepius: Greek god of medicine. Most Roman army doctors seem to have been Greeks.

Avars: Nomadic, horse-riding race from the Central Asian steppes, who conquered Hungary in the 8th century, and clashed with the eastern frontiers of the Frankish Carolingian Empire.

Bactria: Remote eastern region of the ancient Persian Empire, south of the city of Samarkand – a recruiting area for heavy, armoured cavalry.

'Bandage-box': The Latin word *capsarius*, meaning a drum-shaped box for rolled bandages, was also used to mean a Roman medical orderly, who carried one.

'Black Prince': Edward Plantagenet, Prince of Wales, 1330–76; the eldest son of King Edward III of England, he was the victor of many battles against the French, notably Poitiers on 19 September 1356.

'Blitzkrieg': German phrase meaning 'lightning war': a method of overcoming enemy defences by relentless, fast-moving attacks delivered by powerful, self-sufficient columns operating separately and exploiting local success as best they can.

Borodino: Battle in Russia on 7 September 1812, betweeen Napoleon's advancing French and Kutuzov's Russian army. The result was indecisive, even though about 70,000 men fell dead or wounded.

Carbine: Musket or rifle made with a short barrel, for ease of handling on horseback.

Cerignola: Battle in Italy on 26 April 1503, where the Spanish under Gonzalo de Cordoba defeated the French under the Duc de Nemours by the massed fire of hand-gunners entrenched behind a stockade. This was the first decisive victory won by the use of gunnery.

Charlemagne, 742–814: King of the Franks, and from 800, Holy Roman Emperor. A great general and ruler, he created an empire (the 'Carolingian' Empire) stretching out from his capital at Aachen to the Pyrenees in the south-west, half way down Italy in the south-east, and into modern Czechoslovakia in the east.

Cornel wood: Hard type of cherry wood, used to make spear shafts by the Macedonians.

Cornet: In the 17th century, the title of the most junior rank of cavalry officer.

Cossacks: Lightly equipped Russian irregular cavalry, originally descended from Tartar tribesmen.

Crécy: Battle in France on 26 August 1346, when King Edward III of England inflicted a serious defeat on a French army by the use of knights and archers fighting together.

Cromwell, Oliver ('Noll'), 1599–1658: Cavalry leader of Parliament's troops in the English Civil Wars of the 1640s–50s. He rose from captain of a troop to become commander-in-chief, and later ruled England as Lord Protector (military dictator). His sound leadership won such victories as Marston Moor, 1644; Naseby, 1645; and Worcester, 1651.

Crook, Maj. Gen. George, 1892–90: Successful US Army commander during the Indian Wars, particularly the Apache Wars of 1882–86.

Custer, Maj. Gen. George A., 1839–76: Cavalry officer who won an early reputation in the US Civil War, but later became infamous for leading more than 200 men to their deaths at the hands of Indian braves in the battle of the Little Bighorn, 25 June 1876.

Destrier: Norman-French name for a heavy war-horse.

Epona: Ancient Greek goddess, associated with horses and horsemen.

'Goddamns': French nickname for Englishmen during the Hundred Years' War of the 14th and 15th centuries.

Hannibal Barca, 247–183 BC: Carthaginian general who led multi-national armies against the spreading power of the Roman Republic throughout his life, winning many victories and showing tactical genius. Defeated at Zama by the Roman general Scipio in 202 BC, he finally took poison to avoid capture in 183.

Hattin, 'The Horns of': Battle in the Palestinian desert on 4 July 1187, when the great Muslim general Salah al-din ('Saladin') defeated and wiped out an army of Crusaders under Guy of Lusignan.

Jupon: Cloth jerkin worn over torso armour by medieval knights, often embroidered with heraldic designs.

'Mahound': European mis-pronounciation of the prophet Mohammed's name. Ignorant of the Islamic faith, many Crusaders believed that Muslims worshipped the prophet as a pagan god.

Marlborough; John Churchill, 1st Duke of, 1650–1722: English general and diplomat who led allied armies in the War of the Spanish Succession against France in 1701–11. His great victories were Blenheim, 1704; Ramillies, 1706; Oudenarde, 1708; and Malplaquet, 1709. Called by his soldiers 'Corporal John', he followed Cromwell's style of cavalry tactics.

Mesopotamia: That part of the ancient world now occupied by parts of Iraq and Iran, particularly the valleys of the Rivers Tigris and Euphrates.

Numidia: Ancient kingdom in North Africa, roughly modern Algeria, where both Carthage and Rome recruited light irregular cavalry.

Olbia: Greek trading city on the north shore of the Black Sea, where Greeks came in contact with the ancient Scythians.

Pella: The capital of ancient Macedonia, near modern Salonika.

Richard I of England, 1157–99: Nicknamed 'the Lionheart', he led a Crusader army of many nationalities in successful operations during the 3rd Crusade, 1191.

'Scorched earth': The tactic often used by defenders of Russia – or any other region where large areas of empty territory may be given up without disadvantage in order to lure an attacker far from his bases. All crops, animals, and shelter are deliberately destroyed, so that the attackers cannot live off the land.

Seigneurie: Medieval French term, meaning the estates held by an aristocrat.

Steppes: The empty, grassy plains of central Asia, stretching almost without interruption from Hungary to China.

Tyre: Ancient port, now in modern Lebanon, besieged by Alexander the Great in 332 BC.

Varus, Publius Quinctilius: Roman commander whose army of three legions was massacred in Germany in AD 9 at the battle of the Teutoburg Forest — a defeat which discouraged Roman expansion eastwards for generations.

'Vespasian'; Titus Flavius Vespasianus, AD 9–79: Roman general. After campaigns in Germany, Britain, and Palestine, he made himself emperor in the year 69, defeating a rival general at the battle of Cremona.

'The White Death': Nickname given by his Arab enemies to the Byzantine Emperor Nikephoros II Phokas, reigned 963–969.

Xenophon, c. 430–355 BC: Athenian soldier and historian, famous for his book the *Anabasis* – the story of a campaign in which he played a major part as a commander of Greek mercenaries fighting in a Persian civil war.

Zischagge: Type of 17th century cavalry helmet, with an open face guarded by one to three vertical bars, and a laminated 'lobster-tail' neckguard.